The Reunion

by
E.R. Turner

Distributed by:
Granite Publishing and Distribution, L.L.C.
270 S. Mountainlands Dr Suite 7 • Orem, UT 84058
(801) 229-9023 • Toll Free (800) 574-5779
FAX (801) 229-1924

ISBN: 1-57636-051-2
Library of Congress Catalog Card Number: 98-84468
Production by: *SunRise Publishing, Orem, Utah*

For Cathy, without whose encouragement I couldn't have persevered . . . and Dean who said, "You truly captured the reality of life's experiences. I loved the philosophic repartee between Uncle Duane and the guide."

"Everyone must row with the oars he has."
—*old English Proverb*

Characters Reference Guide

Edward/Ila Rose Marsh

Jess/Naomi
1. Ralph Jess/Mary
   1. Ralph
2. Russell/Cora
   Russell/Moira
   1. Robert Jay*
3. Naomi Rose
4. Belle
5. Eddie
6. John

Ralph/Ann (Phil)
1. Elmer
2. Beth Ann

Everett/Minnie
1. Bea
1. Ev
2. Ila May/Theo
2. Sam/Helen
   1. Ted/Penny
   2. Lucyann
   3. Trish
   2. Charlie
   3. Ed/Georgia

Rafe/Maud
1. Ward/Bess
1. Rose/Bradford 2. Ray/Amanda
   (Stewart)
   1. Raphael
2. Martha

Rudy/Martha
1. Roy

Duane/Lucinda
1. David
2. Peter
3. Melissa/Bill
4. Russ
5. *Jay/Darlene
   1. Moira/Dave
      1. Russell Jay
      2. Lucinda
   2. Eddie
   3. Tim

Lulabelle/Neil
(Thomas)
1. Jake/Barbara
2. Amelia Rose

Amos/Maggie Dalrymple
1. Moira
2. Robert

Chapter One

Home

Saturday, August 10th, 10:45 a.m.

Main Street hadn't changed much. A MacDonalds stood on the corner where the mercantile used to be. And behind the school there was a whole new subdivision of houses which, from the size of the trees and shrubs, wasn't more than a year or two old.

"Turn left here," Duane said. Jay knew the way but he didn't say anything. Lately dad had become sensitive about his memory and Jay didn't want to hurt his feelings.

They drove silently for another block. Jay watched his father as they stopped in front of the old home. He was glad it was in good repair even though it had been converted into apartments. The lilacs were gone but the big maple tree was still in the back yard, towering over the house like a watchful parent protecting a child.

"Give me a few minutes please. I want to take a walk around." Jay didn't offer to help. He knew dad needed to take this stroll into his past with only his memories for company.

Duane walked slowly around to the back of the house. The barn, chicken coop and stables had been replaced with a long carport. A white Honda, a rust-scarred Buick and a late-model Ford pickup were in three of the stalls.

When I was here for Lu's funeral eight years ago, Duane thought, *they were just tearing down the barn and remodeling the house into apartments. What a sweet home it was to*

*grow up in. Ma and pa made it come alive with their love
and warmth. Poor pa worried that they couldn't afford to
build it, but with help from his and ma's brothers, and their
own little boys pitching in, somehow it had come into being.*

And then after pa died, ma turned it into a boarding
house for the next seventeen years until her health started to
fail. How she had hated to leave her home and go live with
Lu and Neil. But it was the only thing to do. She hadn't lasted long after the move. She'd just quietly grown more frail
until two years later when Lu checked on her early one
morning and found her lying there peacefully, a calm look on
her face as though she was glad to be with her dear Edward
again.

Duane sighed. *Being the last one is hard,* he thought.
They've all gone now and there's just me left. Even his own
sweet Lucinda had been gone for sixteen years.

It's good to be with my children and their families, he
mused, *but it's time for me to go home now, too.* He glanced
heavenward, "You haven't forgotten about me, have you
Lord? You haven't been too busy to remember I'm still here
have you?"

He smiled to himself. I hope nobody heard me. I'd hate
to have them haul me off to the funny farm. I've got a family
reunion to go to.

Slowly he turned and made his way back around the
house to the car. "Let's go. It's time to join the others."

When they got to the park Duane headed slowly toward
the pavilion.

"Are you okay, grandpa D? Do you need help?" Fifteen-
year-old Eddie bounded out of the back seat and fell into step
with Duane.

Duane smiled at his grandson. "I might be ninety-four
years old, but I'm not helpless yet."

"I know that," Eddie said quickly, "but it's a long trip to here."

Yes, the drive from Flagstaff had been a long one. But it had been wonderful to enjoy the stark beauty of the sandstone and slickrock country around Moab where they stayed last night. And the drive through Monument Valley to Monticello yesterday had been even more beautiful than he'd remembered.

"Creekston is a funny name. Where'd it come from?"

Duane smiled, "The early settlers called it Creek Town because of the creek running through it. I remember them saying it fast running it into one word, pronounced 'Criktown'. By the time I was growing up it had evolved into Creekton." He laughed, "Ma spent a lot of time reminding us kids to pronounce it right."

"When did you leave here? And why did you move to Flagstaff?"

"Let's see. We left Creekston in '46 soon after the war ended. The mines and mills were shutting down and the railroad was being re-routed to the other side of the mountain and I had to find work to support my growing family.

"We went first to Moab and stayed with Jess and his family while I worked on the road crew there. But that only lasted through the summer and fall. Then we moved on to Kanab and stayed with Lucinda's brother for another year and I worked on a construction crew.

"When that ran out I got work in a new lumber mill that had just opened in Flagstaff. I worked there until I retired."

"Did you ever want to move back here?"

"The first few years I did. Most of my family was here. Even Jess came back when he retired. But I love Flagstaff. It's been my home for over forty years. Besides," he put his arm across Eddie's shoulders, "nearly all my children and their children live nearby. I wouldn't give up being around all of you for anything."

"Me too, grandpa D. I'm glad we all live there, too."

They stepped onto the pavilion. "I'm going to get us a table, Eddie. You go on and see your cousins."

Eddie ran toward a group of boys throwing a frisbee at the far end of the pavilion while Duane worked his way to an empty table and waited as Jay and Darlene walked toward him carrying baskets of food.

Relatives were coming by the carloads now. *I wonder if this is how the reunions on the other side will be,* thought Duane, as his nephew Elmer shook his hand warmly and sat beside him on the bench.

"Duane, you look better every time I see you. How do you keep looking so great?"

Duane laughed. "You know Elmer, you sound more like your dad every time I see you. He could charm the scales off a snake."

Elmer grinned. "You always could see right through me." Then he grew thoughtful. "You know, I really can't remember my dad. Sometimes a picture comes into my head and I wonder if I'm remembering him, or just remembering what others have said about him. Was he wild and reckless like they said? Mother never would talk much about him and after she married Phil the memory of dad just seemed to fade away." He looked at Duane. "Don't get me wrong. Phil was a good man and a good father to Beth Ann and me. He just seemed to fill up the space left by dad and we never talked about him again.

"Now I'm old, myself, and expect to meet him again before too many more years." He looked wistful, "I'd kinda like to know what to expect when that time comes."

"Well, don't you go ahead of me! I've already buried

more family than any man ought to have to." Duane continued with a nostalgic note, "Wild and reckless? No, Ralph wasn't really wild and reckless. He was just fearless. And I guess to some people that translates to wild and reckless."

"Fearless? I've never heard anybody say that about him. What do you mean?"

Duane sighed, "Just that. I don't believe he was ever afraid of anything. He was thirteen when I was born so I didn't know him in his early years. But I got to know him real well in the next seventeen years. And the stories I heard ma and pa tell about him around our big kitchen table made me feel I knew him even longer."

Elmer asked quietly, "Then where did he get his reputation? And why did mother always look sad and change the subject when I asked about him? Do you know?"

"Yes. I know. My memories of him have never faded or dimmed. Oh yes, I remember Ralph just as plain as if he was sitting right here with us now."

Chapter Two

Ralph

He pushed the snow away from the mouth of the cave and crawled cautiously out. The small fire in the corner near the opening had gone out before dawn. Now he was cold and stiff. He stood up and stretched his wiry six-foot frame, then pulled his sheepskin coat tighter around him. He looked at the threatening sky. He'd have to get started soon or he'd be snowbound up here and that wasn't part of his plan.

He worked his way down the mountain erratically, some-times stepping from spot to spot carefully and other times leaping into piles of drifted snow with an abandon he found exhilarating.

When he got to the valley floor the snow wasn't as deep so it didn't take him long to reach home. He stamped his feet at the foot of the back steps, then jumped onto the porch and breezed into the kitchen.

"Land sakes, Ralph, where were you last night?"

Ralph looked at his mother. "I told you I was goin' up on the mountain."

"I know," Ila Rose answered, "but I thought sure you'd come back yesterday when the snow started."

"Why would you think that?"

Why indeed? If ever there was a free spirit it was this bright, inquisitive second-born son. From the time he could walk he had explored every inch of every place they'd ever called home. By the time he was nine years old he was camping in the mountains or up the canyons two and three days at a time. Ila Rose and Eddie had learned early on that it didn't do any good to try and fence Ralph in. His need to be totally unrestrained at times couldn't be paddled out of him. And they'd learned to their sorrow that if they tried to put restrictions on him, he'd simply disappear. No, they figured out long ago it was much better to give him a loose rein so he'd at least tell them where he was heading in case he had an accident.

And there had been accidents. He was thrown from a runaway horse that had been spooked by a snake when he was ten years old. He walked on his broken leg and used his broken arm long before the doctor had removed the splints. Then at twelve years of age he'd fallen down an abandoned well and hadn't been discovered for two days. When he was finally pulled up all he said was, "What took you so long?"

By the time he was twenty he'd fallen into a haymow (no one could ever explain how he'd got out of that unscathed), been bucked off a wild horse he was trying to break (the other leg in a splint this time) and fallen under a moving freight train when he was trying to jump into a boxcar. That time he stood up from between the rails after the train had passed with only a sliver in his cheek from the railroad tie his face had pressed against.

In his twenties he'd had fewer, but more perilous, accidents. Caught in the middle of a railroad bridge by an oncoming train he'd jumped to the river sixty feet below. That time his elbow snapped when his arm hit a submerged boulder. Then, just two years ago, he was on a cattle drive when the animals stampeded and he was thrown from his horse. He held onto the reins and was dragged along with the cattle for nearly a mile. Although he was badly bruised over his entire body, he claimed that holding onto the reins saved him from being trampled.

When asked why he got into such awful scrapes his pat answer was always, "A man's gotta do what a man's gotta do without worryin about the consequences. I couldn't survive without my freedom."

Eddie, Jess, the twins and Duane came stomping into the kitchen ready for breakfast, their morning chores completed.

"Good to see you back, Ralph," said Eddie as he looked at his tall, handsome son. "Did you make it to the top?"

"Yep. I could see for miles from there before the storm hit."

As they ate, his brothers watched him with envy. They all stood in awe of this fearless, independent brother.

"Can I go with you next time?" asked fourteen-year-old Duane.

"Sure you can," he smiled. Then he glanced at Ila Rose, her eyes mirroring her unease. "Just as soon as you grow another foot or so."

Duane was crestfallen. "That'll take forever."

"It'll come sooner than you think," laughed Ralph, knowing that when Duane did grow another foot he'd probably also grow enough sense not to want to tag along.

Ralph had never understood his predilection for danger any more than anyone else had. But he did know that, of all the boys in the family, he was the only one gifted with it.

After breakfast Ralph and Eddie put on their coats and walked outside. "We're goin' to check that north fence," Eddie told Ila Rose. "We should be back by noon."

She watched them go, talking quietly together, totally comfortable with each other. Eddie had never shown favoritism among his boys but there was a special bond linking Ralph and him. A bond of trust and loyalty with no strings attached on either side. *Not many dads coulda put up with Ralph's need to run free,* she thought. *I know that I'da*

gone crazy with worry all these years if Eddie hadn't been
here to calm me down and help me accept the way that boy
is.

They walked in silence for awhile. Eddie knew Ralph
had something on his mind. He also knew that when the time
was right he would talk about it.

When they started along the north fence line Ralph said,
"Pa, for some time now I've wanted to ask Annie Parker to
marry me. But I'm not sure I can hack bein' a husband."

"What do you mean?"

"Well, you and ma have had to learn to understand how I
need to get away sometimes. But it took a long time for ma
to get used to it." He laughed good-naturedly, "Even now
that I'm near thirty she still has to remind herself to let go
sometimes.

"Anyway," he went on, "I don't know if it's hard for all
women to let go, and I can't stand the thought of havin' my
freedom gone."

"Have you talked about this with Annie?"

"A little. But not much. I needed time to think about it. I
don't want to ever hurt her."

"Well, she seems like a sensible young woman. And she
don't seem empty-headed and silly like so many of the girls
in town. She's about twenty-four or so, isn't she?"

"She's twenty-five. And you're right, she isn't like most
of the girls around here."

"Do you love her?"

"Yes I do. That's why I don't want to marry her and end
up makin' her life miserable."

"Does she love you?"

"I haven't asked her but I get the feelin' she does."

Eddie smiled. "Well then, it seems like the most sensible
thing to do is talk to each other open and honest. If you both

can live with how you each are, then there shouldn't be a problem, should there?"

Ralph laughed. "I don't know how you always make things seem so simple, pa, but you sure do give a body peace of mind."

* * *

The wedding dance was held in the schoolhouse gym and everybody in town showed up. All the men wanted to dance with the glowing bride and Ralph, in turn, danced with ma, Everett's wife, Minnie, numerous aunts and cousins and five year old Lulabelle. Her eyes shone as she looked up at her big brother smiling down at her like she was a grown up lady herself. The dance lasted nearly all night and Lulabelle was sound asleep long before the couple slipped away for a honeymoon in Bentwood.

Two nights later, the last night of their honeymoon, they enjoyed the festivities in the dining room with the rest of the hotel's patrons. As the bells began to ring Ralph kissed Ann passionately and said "Happy New Year, Mrs. Marsh."

Ann's smile was alive with love. "Happy New Year to you, too, my dearest husband. I hope 1915 will bring you all the joys your heart can hold."

* * *

Spring came in a rush. The days had been cold and stormy then, before anyone realized what was happening, the weather turned warm and flower buds burst through the wet ground in nearly every yard. Daffodils and tulips bloomed in the little flower beds on either side of the steps to the house.

Ann stopped working the soil and sat back on her heels

watching Ralph as he walked along the fence to the gate. "I'm so glad you're back. How was the desert?"

"It was wonderful. I wish you could've gone with me."

"I wish so, too," she patted her stomach, "but Junior wouldn't have liked sleeping on the ground." She stood up and hurried into his outstretched arms.

The real reason she hadn't gone with him was that she knew he was getting restless and needed to get away, alone, for awhile. He had only left once during the winter and that was to trudge on his homemade snowshoes back into one of the canyons for three days. He had tried hard to quiet his agitation but Ann was sensitive to his moods and had encouraged him on both that trip and this past week's jaunt into the desert.

Ralph loved her even more for her concern. He was aware of her perception and discernment and had made every effort to be relaxed and happy at home. Before their marriage she had told him she'd try to understand and they both worked at finding a comfortable middle-ground.

"How have you been while I've been gone? Junior not giving you any problems, is he?"

She laughed. "Not a one. In fact, he's glad when I come outside and dig around the flowers. I can feel his contentment."

And she could. She and Ralph had been so happy when they realized she was pregnant. And though they hadn't discussed it, both of them knew that the root of that contentment was knowing that if anything happened to Ralph, there would always be a reminder of their love to comfort Ann in the years ahead.

Through the summer and fall, Ralph went on a cattle drive, traveled to Spanish Fork for a week where he won five events in the Rodeo there, and joined two other men on a ten-day river run from Jensen to the beautiful wild country south of Moab where the Colorado and Green Rivers meet.

Each time Ann urged him to go and each time she waited fearfully and prayerfully until his safe return home. She had made her peace with his need for these excursions, but it was a tense period for her while he was gone.

By the middle of October he had made his own peace and would not leave again until after the baby came. No matter how assured and calm Ann seemed as she urged him to go, he knew that he could not leave her alone anymore for awhile.

Ann loved every minute of the time Ralph was home. He worked for ranchers and farmers who needed hired hands and he worked for the railroad laying track. He could work these jobs and still be home at night.

Early in the morning three days after Thanksgiving, he hurried across town. "Ma, can you come and help?"

"Is the baby coming?"

"Yes."

Ila Rose smiled. "Do you want Lu to run over and get Annie's ma?"

"I went there first. She's already on her way."

And so Elmer was welcomed into the world by his two grandmas and his daddy. The birth went much easier than the three of them had expected. But Ann wasn't surprised. Her strength had been tempered in the long days waiting for Ralph to come home from his trips. She had already walked through that dark valley of fear and apprehension. With Ralph by her side, holding her hand and tenderly brushing her brow with his cool, strong fingers, she serenely welcomed Ralph's beautiful tiny son into their home.

* * *

Ralph worked in and around Creekston most of the next seven months after Elmer's birth. He took a couple of short trips into the mountains, but was home the rest of the time.

He was fascinated with this tiny son, so helpless yet so bright and quick. He watched the baby nurse, he watched Ann change his diapers and he watched little Elmer grow and develop until he could smile, then laugh, then hold his head up and look around, then sit alone.

"When he's older, I'll teach him all about the mountains and the desert, animals and people," Ralph mused one day as he trotted Elmer on his knee while Ann fixed supper. "I'll take him with me everywhere and he'll learn to love this world like I do."

Ann smiled contentedly. "I'm sure you will. And I'm sure he'll grow up to be just like his daddy." She added playfully, "Do you think you'll do the same thing with his little brother?"

"Brother?" Ralph looked at her in surprise, "Are you in the family way again?"

"Yes," she laughed. "Near as I can tell the new baby should arrive early in the spring."

The July evening was hot so they moved the table and chairs out onto the screened porch in hopes of catching any welcome breeze while they ate.

As they were ready to sit down to supper they heard a strange coughing and sputtering sound coming from above their heads. Ralph picked up the baby and they hurried down the steps in time to see a flying machine pass above the roof of the house.

"What in the world is that?" Ann cried.

Ralph shaded his eyes from the sun. "Why, I believe that's one of those new-fangled aeroplanes."

"I've never heard such a racket before! How does it stay in the air like that?"

He laughed. "I don't know. But I saw that feller, Rodgers, when he flew in his aeroplane across the country four years ago. And his machine sounded even worse than this one."

They watched as the plane flew lower and lower until it came to rest with a bounce and a rattle in Peterson's pasture. Everyone in town had come out of their houses by now and were running toward the pasture.

"Come on, Annie, let's go look, too."

She was a little afraid of the noisy contraption but she hurried to keep up with him. When they got to the pasture a man was climbing down from the plane. The townspeople formed a wide circle around him, looking fearfully at this thing that had come out of the sky into their midst.

"Howdy," called the stranger, "I hope I didn't scare you. It's getting on to evening and I didn't dare fly any further when I saw those mountains ahead." He looked at the astonished faces. "Don't be afraid. You can see it won't hurt you."

People slowly walked nearer, some reaching out to touch the plane. He held up his hand. "It's better if you don't touch it just yet. I want to make sure the engine's cooled down first. Then if you'll come one at a time, those who want to can touch it. But be careful. I'll have a hard time flying out of here tomorrow if you break anything."

As the crowd surged forward Ann studied Ralph's expression as he handed Elmer to her and started toward the plane. *Oh no,* she thought, *he's got that look on his face. Please don't want to ride in that thing. It looks like it'll fall apart any minute.*

Soon Ralph and the stranger were deep in conversation. They talked of Rodger's flight and the failure of the American air expedition against Mexican bandits two years ago and how aeroplanes were being used in the war in

Europe even now. They both kept a close watch on the plane while a few people reached out and cautiously touched this strange flying machine.

"Ann, come and meet Mr. Perkins."

"Please, call me Matt."

"Matt, this is my wife, Ann. Annie, this is Matt Perkins, the driver of this beautiful aeroplane." The longing in Ralph's voice was not lost on Ann.

"How do you do, Mr. Perkins." She smiled, "I suspect you could use something to eat. Why don't you come home and have supper with us."

Ralph's smile was broad with joy. "Let's step over there and ask Lars if you can park your aeroplane here tonight. I'm sure he won't mind."

By the time the arrangements were agreed to, most of the people had wandered back to their own houses and suppers still talking about new-fangled machines that could actually fly like birds.

"Where did you come from in your aeroplane, Mr. Perkins?" Ann looked at him solemnly.

"I left four days ago from Marysville, Kansas but I set down in both Nebraska and Colorado along the way here." He laughed. "I am in Utah now, aren't I?"

They joined in his laughter. "Yes. I guess up there in the sky a man can't see when he's crossin' the border from one state to the next, can he? Where're you headin' from here?" Ralph's eyes were alive with interest.

"I'm hoping to make it as far as Carson City in Nevada, then I'll work my way back home again on a more southern course so I can fly over as much of the country as possible. My plane'll need an overhaul soon but I hope to do that at home where I've got all the parts I need."

"How'd you get started flyin'?"

Matt leaned back in his chair with a faraway expression on his face. "I was born in Grandy, North Carolina. When I was ten years old my family moved in with my grandparents in Kitty Hawk while my dad recuperated from an accident he'd had on our farm."

He sighed. "I'll never forget that day. It was the 17th of December. We'd all heard about the Wright brothers who'd been experimenting with gliders. Most folks thought they were crazy.

"Anyway, word got around that they were going to try and fly a glider propelled by an engine. I ran with some of the other boys in town out to the dunes where they were. I'll never forget seeing that machine actually fly in the air. It only lasted a few seconds but I resolved then that as soon as I was big enough I was going to fly, too. And now I do. However," he smiled ruefully, "this is the farthest I've flown so far."

The fire in Matt's eyes was transported to Ralph whose face took on a look of pure rapture. It was obvious that to fly among the clouds would be the culmination of everything he'd ever done or wanted to do.

He glanced across at Ann and saw the concern in her eyes. He smiled reassuringly at her then turned and asked Matt, "What're your plans when you get back home? Will you be out this way again?"

"Not for awhile," was the reply. "The war in Europe is escalating and I'm convinced we'll be in it by next year. I'm going to offer my plane and my services to the army so I can be doing what I love when we finally get involved over there."

As Ann watched, Matt seemed to already be a part of the future. And Ralph's look wasn't far behind. "I guess if we do go to war I'll have to think about joinin' up, too."

"No!" Ann cried involuntarily, putting her hand to her mouth. But the fire of battle was already glowing in the eyes of both men and they seemed impervious to her distress. She braced herself, trying for the strength and courage she had maintained so far in their marriage. In a steady voice she asked, "Are you ready for cake?"

They nodded and kept talking as Ann turned from the table and walked to the shelf where the cake sat waiting. Please, dear God, don't let Ralph go to war, she prayed as she cut slices of cake and put them on plates. I couldn't bear to have him so far away and in such danger. With your help I've been able to abide his need for adventure here close to home, but I couldn't stand to have something happen to him so far away.

She molded her expression into a look of serenity as she carried the plates of cake to the table. *I promised I wouldn't tie Ralph down,* she reflected, *so I'll keep my thoughts and my worries to myself.*

After supper Ann put the baby in his crib in the bedroom and did the dishes as she listened to the men converse. They talked of the war and of the kinds of planes now in service.

"The De Havilland and the Sopwith Camel and the Handley Page the English are using are working pretty good but, in addition to their Gothas, the Germans have added a new plane to their flying force called the Junkers that is a much better plane.

"I read just before I came on this trip that a Dutchman by the name of Fokker has invented a machine gun that can fire between the propeller blades as a plane flies. If that's true it will make aeroplanes real fighting machines."

"Imagine that," said Ralph, "aeroplanes that can actually shoot at each other. What I wouldn't give to see somethin' like that!"

Enough of this, thought Ann, *I can't listen to any more.* "Mr. Perkins, our house isn't much but if you don't mind we'll be glad to make you a bed out on the back porch and you can sleep there tonight. We don't have a hotel here in town."

Ralph added, "In all the excitement I'm forgettin' my manners, Matt. You're more than welcome to sleep here tonight."

"Thanks, I appreciate the offer. But I always sleep out by my plane when I'm flying. I've got a bedroll stashed away under the seat and I'll pull that out and be quite content." He laughed, "I've got so used to sleeping out under the stars I'm not sure I'd be able to get to sleep anywhere else. But thanks anyway."

He looked at the clock in the corner. "It's getting late. I'd better head out and let you people get your sleep."

"You're welcome to stay longer," Ralph said wistfully, anxious to hear more.

Matt smiled, "I appreciate that but I'm hoping to get an early start in the morning so I'd better go."

"Here," said Ralph as he picked up a lantern, "I'll go along with you. It's pretty dark out there tonight."

"Thanks," Matt turned to Ann, "and thanks again for supper Mrs. Marsh. I've enjoyed this evening here with you good people."

She smiled and nodded as the two walked out the door. Whatever happens, she mused as the men walked down the steps and into the night, I've got to stay positive and pleasant. I knew what Ralph was when I married him and he was honest enough to tell me about his need to be free. I'll not start buying trouble now. I'll just wait and take what comes. I won't try to tie Ralph to me with tears or nagging. I love him too much for that.

She sat in the rocking chair and watched little Elmer through the bedroom door as he slept peacefully in his crib.

She dozed there awhile until Ralph ran up the steps and into the house. He grabbed her up from the chair and whirled her around the room as he exclaimed, "Matt's takin me for a ride in his aeroplane in the mornin' before he leaves!"

His happiness was so infectious Ann could only smile at him and nod. There was no way she'd put a damper on his joy.

* * *

Ann looked around carefully. Ralph was seated at her side, smiling broadly. She was holding a baby on her lap and Elmer was sitting snugly on the seat between them. As far as she could see there was nothing but blue—the clearest, most beautiful blue she had ever seen. She peered high above and saw the blue deepening to blackness in the distance but she was not afraid.

Out of the corner of her eye she spied something white; something so small it was barely visible. She turned to watch it and was amazed as the brightness grew and expanded until it filled the space around them. It was warm and quiet within the white mist and very comforting.

Then they flew out of the white and into the blue again. She turned to look at Ralph and saw such a look of pleasure she wanted to reach out and touch him. But she couldn't move her arms which were encircling the baby and Elmer. Ralph turned and smiled at her and in that instant she knew that her expression, too, was filled with pure delight. That was what she felt — pure, unrestrained pleasure and freedom.

I never knew, she thought. *This must be what Ralph feels when he frees himself from the mundane. There's a taste and a sense and a touch of immortality.* She leaned back contentedly.

Suddenly there was a jolt and a sharp crack, then a loud rattling sound. She looked quickly at Ralph.

He smiled calmly and said, "I'm goin' to take us over to that cloud. When we get there you take the children and climb out."

"But a cloud can't keep us from falling."

"That one can. Trust me. you must climb out when I tell you."

"But what will you do?"

"I'll fix what's wrong and come back for you."

So she gathered up the little ones and stepped out of the plane and onto the cloud. Ralph blew her a kiss and flew away, the plane's racket growing louder.

Suddenly the plane gave a great shudder and began twisting and turning slowly toward the ground. Ann watched from her perch as the plane grew smaller and smaller.

Instantly she was standing on the ground watching as the plane fell toward her. It hit the ground with a soft sigh and, in slow motion, broke into pieces which immediately crumbled into dust. She ran over to where it had fallen. Ralph was standing just above the settling remains smiling lovingly at her.

She felt the same calm she had felt when they were in the plane together earlier. He continued to smile at her then waved, turned and began climbing stairs only he could see.

She reached out her hand to him. "Don't go, Ralph!" she cried. "Please don't go yet!"

But he walked on without a backward glance.

"Ralph! Ralph! Please come back! Please don't leave!"

Strong hands gently shook her shoulders. "Wake up,

Annie. Wake up. You're havin' a nightmare."

His words brought instant tranquility and she pressed her face against his chest. She could feel the steady beat of his heart. He was here in bed with her! Her dear Ralph hadn't gone!

"Oh, Ralph, I love you so much," she whispered.

He kissed the top of her head. "And I love you, little Annie. I always will."

They fell asleep in each other's arms.

* * *

It was a half hour before sunrise when Ralph held Ann in his arms and gave her a lingering kiss. "I gotta go, Annie. He'll be waitin' for me."

She clung to him, the words bursting from her mouth in spite of her good intentions. "Please don't go, Ralph! I just don't feel good about this!"

"It was only a dream, Annie, a silly nightmare."

"I know that, Ralph. But I just have a strange feeling about you going up in that machine today."

He looked at her serious, worried expression. "Okay, Annie girl, if it means that much to you, I'll go tell him I'm not goin' after all." Try though he might, he couldn't keep the disappointment from his voice.

"Oh Ralph," she wiped her eyes. The memory of the contentment and awe she'd felt in the air during her dream flooded over her. "I'm sorry. I know how much this ride means to you. Don't pay any attention to me. I'm just being foolish." She forced a smile and embraced him tightly. "Go on now, he's waiting for you."

He gazed deeply at her. "I truly do love you, Annie. Don't worry. I'll be back here with you before you know it."

He walked down the steps then turned, "I'll have him fly over the house and we'll wave at you. Watch for us."

Oh yes, thought Ann, *I'll watch and pray and hold tight to the thought of your safe return every minute you're gone.*

She went back inside preparing herself to keep busy every minute, her proven survival formula whenever Ralph was off on one of his adventures.

In a very short time she heard the rattle and cough of the aeroplane drawing near. She ran outside, waving a dishtowel as the plane passed overhead, Ralph laughing and waving as they headed west.

"I've done a lot of things in my life," yelled Ralph over the noise of the engine, "but this tops them all!"

Matt nodded, understanding exactly what Ralph was feeling. Every aviator comprehended the pull of the heavens to those whose feet were not content to remain on solid ground.

"That's Bentwood," Ralph mouthed and pointed. They flew low over the county seat watching with amusement as people came rushing outside to see this marvelous contraption flying overhead.

After Bentwood they flew west another twenty miles then angled the plane northward. Ralph called out the names of each town as they passed over it. He'd been to all of them within this radius but each one presented another perspective from the air.

Oh, how Ann would love this, he thought. *I'm goin' to learn to fly, too, so I can take her up here like a bird.*

Then it came time to head back. The harmony of the earth and the sky blended into one great whole. The noise of the engine seemed to fade as the glory of flight grew and expanded. Conversation wasn't necessary. They both reveled in the experience. Soon they were flying again over

Bentwood. Once again people came out to wave and stare.

As the plane climbed over the rise east of town, it gave a slight lurch. Undisturbed, Ralph glanced at Matt who was busy pushing and pulling and twisting and turning levers. Matt knew what he was doing. There was nothing to worry about.

The plane shook again, stronger this time.

* * *

Ann stopped scrubbing. What had she heard? She listened intently. Nothing. *Only my imagination.*

Before she could reach into the sudsy bucket for the brush, it came again, not so much a sound as a feeling. She hurried outside. The breeze rustled the leaves in the big cottonwood tree back of the house but that was the only sound. Then, distantly, in the direction of Bentwood there came a faint sort of whine. Then a muffled whumph like the sound of dynamite when they were blasting at the quarry.

Ann walked slowly back into the house. She picked up Elmer and held him tightly. She sat in the rocking chair, an unusual feeling enveloping her. A feeling of calm and peace. The room seemed to lighten. *The sun must have come out from behind a cloud,* she thought, then knew instinctively that wasn't it at all.

She sat quietly cuddling Elmer, slowly rocking back and forth. Excited voices permeated the silence but couldn't penetrate Ann's sense of tranquility.

"Ann! Ann! Are you home?" Footsteps hurried across the porch and the screen door swung open. He stepped into the kitchen and stood silently. Slowly he walked toward her.

Ann looked up at him from the rocker and smiled gently at his ravaged face. "I know, Eddie, I know."

She gently placed Elmer on the floor and walked into her father-in-law's outstretched arms.

* * *

"Mama, Uncle Duane's here!" Eight-year-old Elmer ran and threw his arms around Duane's waist.

"How nice to see you, Duane. When did you get back?" Ann reached up and kissed his cheek.

"About an hour ago. As soon as I could I hurried over here to see my best pal." He threw Elmer over his broad shoulders and carried him piggy-back into the kitchen. Six-year-old Beth Ann shyly peeked her head out from behind her mother's skirt.

"Come here, Bethie. See what I brought for you." Duane squatted down to release Elmer.

With both children standing excitedly in front of him he reached into his shirt pockets and brought out a pocketknife and a tiny porcelain doll.

"If you can guess which one is for you," he looked at each child in turn, "you get to keep it."

Elmer shrieked with joy. "I know, Uncle Duane! I know! The knife is for me!"

Duane turned to Beth Ann. "Is he right?" She nodded shyly.

"Then which one is for you?" She pointed to the doll, her eyes alive with pleasure.

"Oh, you are both too smart for me. Here you go." He gave the children their prizes.

"Will you have supper with us?" Ann asked softly.

"Yes, thanks."

After the supper dishes were done Ann and Duane sat out on the front porch and talked quietly while the children played with their new toys. There had always been mutual respect and love between them but after Ralph's death, Duane had tried to fill the children's lives with some of the love their father had given to him when he was growing up.

"How was the job?"

Duane smiled. "You know, I hated to leave Creekston, but I really did enjoy the cattle drive and visiting Denver. And I met a pretty little filly there who promised to answer my letters if I wrote to her." He laughed mischievously, "So I sent her a letter from every town on the way home."

Ann laughed. "And was there any mail waiting here for you?"

"Yep. Answers to every letter she'd received."

"Does that mean you might be moving to Denver?" A touch of nostalgia crossed her face.

"No. The beauty of it is her folks are moving to Salt Lake next year." He hesitated. "I guess we'll just have to see what happens then."

"Well, I'm so glad for you. You're a good man, Duane."

"Now I don't know about that but I hear tell you've met someone special, Ann."

"Yes," she answered hesitantly, knowing the love Duane had always had for Ralph. "I never planned to marry again. Ralph was the only man I thought I ever wanted. But I'm finding Phil looking better all the time. And he's so good to the children."

"That's just great. I'm glad for you, Ann. And I think Ralph would want you to marry again, too."

They sat in comfortable silence for awhile. "You've never talked about Ralph. And you took his death so calmly. I'm not trying to pry, but are you okay, Ann?"

"Yes, I'm fine. I haven't talked about him because what we had was so special I've held it in my heart all this time, filling myself with his goodness and his memory. He's been here with me so often. Sometimes I feel him so close I know if I reach out I can almost touch him."

She continued quietly, "I knew he wouldn't be with us long. I sensed it from the first. And then, just before he died, the feeling was so strong, yet so peaceful, that to mourn him would have been a mockery of the love we shared. So I've just kept him locked in my heart and not even talked about him to the children much.

"But now I feel strongly that he wants me to give his children a father again and he wants me to love that father. Phil isn't Ralph and I don't expect him to be. And he won't be taking Ralph's place. No one could ever do that. But I think soon it'll be time for him to become part of our lives. He's been real good and never tried to rush my feelings. Maybe that's why I'm ready to love again."

Duane put his arm around her shoulders and the two of them sat comfortably in the dusk remembering, yet watching as another door opened ahead for them.

Chapter Three

Doors

Saturday, August 10th, 11:05 a.m.

They sat quietly for a few minutes. "Thanks Duane. You've opened a door for me to pass through and find my dad again."

"He was a good man, Elmer. Perhaps he shouldn't have taken so many chances, but who's to know what's right for another person? He lived the only way he could, I believe."

"Yes," Elmer smiled, "I think so, too."

They watched as more relatives arrived. "Is that your boy over there beckoning to you?"

Elmer looked in the direction Duane was pointing. "Yes. I guess they're getting ready to eat. Thanks again, Duane. You always were special to me. And I know mother always had a special place in her heart for you."

They shook hands again, lingering over the physical contact. "Just remember not to go leaving this world before I do," Duane said with a twinkle in his eyes as Elmer walked away.

"Uncle Duane, how are you?"

Duane looked up into the smiling face of Lu's daughter. "Why Amelia Rose, how nice to see you!"

He stood and embraced her warmly. "Come and sit and visit awhile. It's so good to see you."

She sat by his side. "It's so good to see you, too. It's been way too long." She laughed, "But we say that at every reunion, don't we."

"Tell me about you and your family. Are they all here with you today?"

"Most of them. My oldest grandson and his wife are back east in school so they won't be here."

Another door we can't go back through, Duane thought as he said, "It seems impossible you're old enough to have married grandchildren."

"Seems that way to me, too. I don't know where the years went." She looked steadily at Duane, "You're looking good. Do you feel as good as you look?"

He laughed, "I guess you could say I'm in good shape for the shape I'm in."

"You sounded just like mama then," she laughed. "Dad always said all the Marsh's had a great sense of humor."

"Oh, we had some wonderful times. And your dad was always a real special part of our family."

"He always felt that way, too. I'm glad to have come from such good people. I wouldn't call mother and dad back for the world but sometimes I miss them both so much."

"Yes," Duane said quietly, "I know what you mean. I miss them, too."

Amelia Rose saw a hint of sadness pass quickly across his features. "Have you driven over to the old home yet?"

"Yes, I had Jay drive over there on our way here this morning. Do you remember much about it?"

"Not a lot. I was only four when grandma died. I remember years later feeling like a door closed after she was gone, leaving all of us on the other side."

She smiled nostalgically, "Mama used to talk about that home a lot. She loved it. And she loved Creekston. I remember her telling me once that of all the places she'd ever been, Creekston was the dearest."

"Well, Lu learned, like we all have to, that sometimes the most precious things are right under our own noses."

Chapter Four

Lulabelle

"Lu! Lu! Lulabelle! Where has that dratted girl disappeared to now?" Ila Rose turned to Neil, "She was here just a minute ago. Do you want to wait while I go look for her?"

"No. I've got to get to work." He smiled at Jake who was piling more hotcakes onto his plate. "Bye, son. Don't be late for school."

Before turning to leave he said, "Ila Rose, will you just remind Lu about the meeting at school tonight."

Ila Rose nodded as Neil left. *Sure, I'll remind her,* she thought, *but she won't be anxious to go. Lu don't never want to go anywhere 'cept parties and dances. And a P.T.A. meetin' don't even come close.*

Ila Rose thought about her only daughter. Lulabelle had come along late in life, ten years after Duane, the youngest of their six boys, and maybe they had given in to her too often. Eddie had warned all of them they were spoiling Lu, but even he'd had a soft spot for this happy, fun loving daughter. She'd always been such a beauty, and bright as a whip.

Ila Rose reflected, *maybe not bright so much as artful.* Lulabelle had got everything she wanted from the time she was a baby. And marrying Neil hadn't slowed her down at all.

They'd all hoped being the wife of gentle, good hearted Neil would mellow Lu out. But it hadn't. Even after Jake was born she'd bounced right back to her flirtatious, flighty ways.

Ila Rose smiled. *Trouble is,* she thought, *everybody likes Lu just the way she is. Especially Neil.*

"Now Bert, let go of me. I gotta get back or ma'll be comin' out to look for me."

"Oh hell, Lu. Your ma knows you'll be back. Quit worryin'."

Lulabelle smiled and leaned forward. "Well, maybe one little kiss. Then I gotta go."

They were in the niche where the chicken coop abutted the side of the barn. Nobody could see them here. *And a little kiss once in awhile ain't gonna hurt anybody,* Lulubelle thought. A girl's gotta have some fun, even if she is married.

Humming, she did the two-step as she headed for the back door of the two story frame house her ma had turned into a boarding house after pa died. Once inside Lu put the basket of eggs on the table and picked up Jake's empty dishes and carried them to the sink.

Lu came every morning at five to help ma cook breakfast for the boarders. Neil got Jake up and ready for school and dropped him off to have breakfast in ma's big, sweet smelling kitchen before heading to school. This morning Jake had finished his mush and hotcakes and was already gone. Lu didn't worry about him. Ma always made sure he left for school on time whether Lu was around or not.

Lu loved Jake. And she loved Neil. She just didn't see why she should stop having a good time just cause she was a happily married mama. Life went by too fast anyway. She'd be twenty-five on her next birthday and she could still tempt any man in town with her big, black, lustrous eyes and merry laugh. Life was for living to the fullest and she meant to get everything out of it she could before she got old like some of the old biddies in town.

"Did Jake get off to school okay, ma?"

Nodding, Ila Rose looked at her daughter's mischievous smile and the bright smear of lipstick streaked across her cheek. "My laws, Lu! Go clean your face."

Lu walked to the cracked mirror hanging by the back door and wiped her cheek with the back of her hand. She turned around with a grin. "I guess I musta rubbed against somethin'."

"Yes, I guess you did. I just hope Bert's wife don't notice he rubbed against the same thing." She watched Lu's dancing eyes. "I saw him come sneakin' round the barn as you was comin' in the door just now."

Lulabelle laughed. "Oh ma, she's so dumb. He'd just tell her he'd been eatin' strawberries and she'd believe him." She added, "There's nothin' wrong with havin' a little fun before you get old and gray and the men don't look at you no more."

"Just make sure it is just a little fun. Jake don't deserve a harlot for a ma. And Neil don't deserve to be married to one."

Lulabelle's eyes grew large. "Why ma! What a thing to say! You know I don't let anybody get the best of me! But a little kiss once in awhile don't hurt nothin'."

"Let's hope not. You still oughta think about somebody besides yourself once in awhile."

"Why, I think about other people all the time!" She laughed. "I think about Bert and Sam and Nate and..."

"Stop! I don't want to hear anymore. Besides, you know what I mean."

"Yeah, ma. I know what you mean. I wouldn't hurt Jake or Neil for the world. But Neil knew I was a flirt when he married me. That's why he kept comin' back until I finally said yes. And Jake," she hesitated. "Well, he's growin' up just fine. He knows I love him." She laughed, "And besides, he can outsmart any kid in school even though he's only in the third grade. So don't worry about him."

"Oh, I don't worry about him gettin' along. He's so much like you it scares me sometimes. But I guess that's okay. I see Neil look at him with such pride and love sometimes. Just like he looks at you."

Lulabelle responded seriously, "I know, ma. I see the same thing. And Jake loves his pa somethin' fierce. I really wouldn't do anythin' to hurt either of them. I just want to have some fun while I'm still young enough to enjoy it."

Next morning Ila Rose had already gathered the eggs so Lulabelle stayed in the kitchen and helped with the cooking. When Neil brought Jake in he ran over and hugged his mama tight before sitting down to breakfast.

"You look mighty fetching this morning, Lu," said Neil as she threw her arms around him. "Wish I didn't have to go to work today."

Grinning temptingly she winked and replied, "Me, too."

With a sigh he said, "I better get going. Jobs are too hard to come by and I can't afford for me to lose this one just cause I've got the prettiest wife in five counties."

As the screen door shut behind him, Ila Rose said, "Lu, you go ahead and sit down and have breakfast with your boy."

"But ma, you said you got a new boarder last night. That means more work with an extra mouth to feed this mornin'."

"It's okay. I've got everythin' ready. You sit down right there and eat with Jake."

Lu didn't see the concerned look on Ila Rose's face as she carried the heavy tray into the dining room. The new boarder wasn't like the cowpokes around here. He was smooth talking and flashy and she didn't want Lu tempted beyond repair. It was one thing for her to flirt with the men here in town. Every one of them knew she liked to tease but that was as far as it went. And they all liked and respected Neil. They'd never push things too far with Lulabelle. But Mr. Butch Jones (if that was his real name she'd eat her hat) wasn't going to sweet-talk Lulabelle if Ila Rose could help it.

She watched him work his charm as he ate with the others. He was a good six feet tall and had light brown hair, a wide intelligent face and an ever smiling mouth. But there was a look in his darting brown eyes that put Ila Rose on her guard. Even as old as she was, she could feel his magnetic masculinity. *I'm afraid,* Ila Rose thought, *there's more there than meets the eye.*

"Where you from Mr. Jones?" asked Bill Kirby. "You don't talk like you're from around here."

"Call me Butch," he answered as he looked around the table. "Well now, I'm from all over. I was born in St. Louis but I've been traveling so long with my work that I guess I could call the whole U.S. of A. my home."

"What work do you do?" spoke up Jess Cassidy.

"Why, I check out land for a big corporation in New York City and get all the financial deals done so it can be developed and sold to investors."

"You'll have a hard time findin' any decent land round here. All we got's sagebrush and alkali. The crick's the only water we got and some years even that's not enough for growing much."

Butch's expression turned serious and, looking into each pair of eyes candidly, said, "You'd be surprised how much my company has learned about finding water underground where no one ever thought there'd be any. We've developed some pretty dry parcels of land into veritable Gardens of Eden."

"Well, good luck tryin' that here," said Bill. "This ain't

no Eden and even our gardens are purty sickly some of the time."

"I'll know about that after I've looked around for awhile."

Ila Rose carried the empty tray back into the kitchen in time to give Jake a quick kiss before he left for school.

"You look kinda tired, ma. Why don't you relax while I go in and start gathering up the dirty dishes."

Ila Rose stood quickly. "No, Lu, I need you more here in the kitchen. I'm plannin' some pies for supper and I need you to help me with 'em."

Lulabelle looked at ma incredulously. Ma always started on the supper baking while Lu cleaned up the dining room. "Okay," she said reluctantly, "but I can help in both places, you know."

"Yes. I know. I'd just like it if you got the table in here cleaned up and ready and start rollin' the dough for me this time."

They both turned around with a start as the dining room door flew open and banged into the wall.

"Oops, excuse me. I didn't realize the door opened so fast." Butch Jones stood there with a hang-dog look. But his eyes didn't look remorseful, Ila Rose noticed.

"What do you want?" she asked brusquely. "I don't like people comin' in my kitchen."

"Oh, I am sorry. I didn't know. I was just leaving when I remembered I'd forgot to ask you when supper is served. I don't want to cause any trouble being late." He didn't add that he'd overheard some of the men talking about Lulabelle's beauty and when he'd asked they told him she was Ila Rose's daughter and helped her ma in the kitchen every morning.

You don't want to cause trouble all right, thought Ila

Rose angrily, *then why did you come in here?* "I told you last night that supper is at 6 p.m. sharp."

Butch looked perplexed. "I am truly sorry. I don't recollect that at all, ma'am." His eyes shifted boldly to Lulabelle who stood transfixed.

"Well, the time hasn't changed. You better go now. We got work to do." Ila Rose was determined not to introduce him to Lu.

He hesitated briefly then grinned and walked out of the room. Ila Rose shut the door firmly.

"Who's that, ma? Why didn't you introduce me?"

"He's nobody you want to know. He won't be around here long."

"Even so, you could have introduced me. Is he the new boarder? He's mighty fine lookin'."

"Handsome is as handsome does. Let's get busy. He's taken up too much of our time already. Come on, we can't stand here talkin' about him any longer."

Ma seems awful upset, thought Lu, *I wonder why?* She rolled the dough and hummed quietly as she reflected on the dancing eyes and brilliant smile she had found so exciting.

By the middle of the afternoon the kitchen was cleaned up, the pies were baking and the dining room table was set for supper.

"You go on home now, Lu. I appreciate your help but you got your own housework to do before Jake gets home from school."

Lulabelled hugged Ila Rose. "You been real quiet today, ma. If you're worried about me flirtin' with your new boarder, you can put your mind at ease. I might enjoy a little funnin' with the town men but that's all. I'm not about to bite off more than I can chew."

She stopped in at the mercantile to buy some peppermints for Jake. He always enjoyed finding a treat when he got home from school.

As she turned the corner to go up the lane to her house a movement in the shadows of the elm tree by the canal caught her eye. "Who's there?"

"Don't be afraid, ma'am. It's just me." He stepped forward onto the path.

"What are you doin' here?"

"Why, I'm just checking on this property. Do you know who owns it?" He put out his hand, "Bye the way, my name is Butch Jones and I'd be pleased to make your acquaintance."

Lulabelle looked at his hand but didn't take it. "I know your name already."

He seemed surprised. "For goodness sakes. I almost didn't recognize you. I saw you this morning in your mother's kitchen, didn't I? You're Lulabelle." His beautiful white teeth flashed in a luxuriant smile.

Lu was mesmerized. She couldn't force her gaze from his face. She was sure if she tried to move she'd find herself unable to do so. She'd never before met anyone so fascinating, anyone who had such power over her. She felt herself being drawn into a perilous sphere from which there was no escape.

"Do you live nearby?" His voice was rich and full and held promises of wonderful things to come.

"My house is right up the path." Lulabelle's voice quivered as she answered. All her fine sounding talk to ma earlier came flooding back, "I don't let anybody get the best of me...not about to bite off more than I can chew...."

And then her mother's face, clear and concerned, came into her mind breaking the spell. "Excuse me, Mr. Jones." Her voice was strong and firm, "I've got work to do."

Without a backward glance she swept past him and marched solidly on up the path. He stood very still, watching her.

"You're a beauty all right," he murmured, "but you're still a country bumpkin. I'll bide my time. You'll be eating out of my hand, yet, miz Lulabelle."

The encounter on the path plagued Lu's waking hours and intruded upon her dreams. The aura of mystery and intrigue about Butch Jones was so strong she could find no peace. She had never met anyone like him.

"You've been awful quiet lately, Lu. Is something the matter?"

Lu and Neil sat on the porch after supper enjoying the sweet scented May evening. The sense of goodness and decency surrounding Neil was palpable. *I'll never do anythin' to hurt him,* Lu thought. *Never.* She'd kept very busy the past three days since the confrontation with Mr. Jones. She was determined not to be near him again.

"Lu?"

"What? Did you say somethin'?"

"Are you feeling all right? You look kinda pale."

She forced herself to keep her gaze steady on his dear face. "I'm fine. Don't worry about me." She leaned her head on his shoulder. "You're a good man, Neil, and I love you."

He carefully studied his wife, the only woman he had ever loved. Something was bothering her but he wouldn't pry. When she was ready she'd tell him about it. "I love you, too, Lulabelle. I always have. And you know I'll always be here for you."

"I know, Neil. I know." *I won't let myself think about white, shining teeth and flashing brown eyes! I won't!*

But the next day as Lulabelle turned up the path leading home again, there under the elm tree stood the man she was trying so hard to forget. "Well, Lulabelle, we meet again."

"What are you doin' here?"

His smile was the only answer he gave. "You've been avoiding me. Now why would you do that?" His sensuality was overwhelming.

Lu took a step back. She compelled herself to look away from his hypnotic gaze. "Please get out of my way and leave me alone, Mr. Jones."

He laughed. "Are you sure that's what you really want? Are you sure you want me to leave you alone?"

No, her heart whispered. No, I don't want you to leave me alone. I want to be with you. She looked down without a word.

"If that's what you really want, I'll leave you alone." She looked up quickly. His eyes were shrewd as he gave her a lop sided grin. "But first, tell me who owns the property at the top of that rise there."

Lulabelle looked at the hill behind her house. "Neil's Uncle Ross."

"Neil?"

"My husband."

There was an expectant silence. "This Uncle Ross— would he sell that parcel of land?"

Lulabelle laughed. "Sell it? Whatever for? It's not good for anything. It's just dry, parched dirt and rocks."

Butch frowned. "It has promise. I've walked all over that rise and I believe my employers could make something of it."

"Your employers?"

"The corporation I work for. The people they deal with would be glad to invest in some land out here."

Lu felt herself being pulled again into the magnetism of this man. She shook her head to clear it. "I'll ask Uncle Ross. But now I've got to go."

The following Monday Lulabelle found Butch Jones waiting for her once again. "Did you find out about that piece of land, yet?"

She swallowed the lump in her throat. "He might be interested. You can ask him yourself. He lives in the third house down from the mercantile."

Lulabelle turned to go but he took hold of her arm. "Take just a minute and walk with me up there. There's some rocks that look like they've got Indian writing on them."

She knew the rocks he was talking about. What harm can it do to go with him, she persuaded herself, nothin' can happen this close to home.

They climbed up past sagebrush and boulders. When they got to the top they walked toward the rocks he'd asked about. Pointing, he asked, "Is it Indian writing?"

"Everybody says so. We had some students from the college up in Salt Lake out here lookin' at them last year. But we haven't heard any more from them."

She looked around her. She'd forgotten how isolated this spot was. She realized he was looking at her intensely.

"I gotta go."

But before she could take a step he gathered her in his arms and kissed her. She forgot all her vows and promises to stay away from him. She threw her arms around his neck and returned his kiss fervently. They stood locked in each others arms.

Butch whispered, "I knew it would be like this, Lu. This was meant to be, you know."

She was speechless, her head against his chest. The fire in her was consuming every shred of resistance. He kissed her again.

After a long while she pulled away from him. "This is wrong," she whispered. "I can't stay here any longer."

And with an overpowering sense of shame mixed with elation she hurried back down the hill and into the house. She leaned against the door thinking, *what have I done? What have I done?*

She spent a sleepless night. The next morning Ila Rose looked hard at her and said, "What's wrong, Lu?"

"Nothin' ma."

"You look downright sick. You better go home and lay down."

"No," Lulabelle responded quickly, "I can't go home. I need to be here and help you."

Ila Rose didn't say any more but she stole worried glances at Lu every little while. Finally she could stand it no longer.

"Lu, that's the third time you've washed that plate. Tell me what's the matter."

"There's nothin' to tell, ma." Lu looked around unseeingly. She tried to laugh but the ensuing sound was nearer a sob. "Maybe you're right, ma. Maybe I should go home. Maybe I'm comin' down with somethin'."

Ila Rose looked at her sharply. She'd never seen Lulabelle like this. "Maybe you are comin' down with somethin'. Go on home and rest." She paused then added, "Do you need me to come with you?"

"No, ma, no! I'll be fine. I just need to lay down awhile."

Lulabelle hurried down the street. She didn't stop at the mercantile for a sweet for Jake. She couldn't think straight about anything. She slowly climbed the porch steps.

"Lu!"

She turned. Butch came hurrying toward her. "I talked to Ross. He's willing to sell."

She looked at him blindly. "Please go," she whispered. "Please leave me alone."

"Is that what you really want?" he said tenderly as he cupped her chin in his hand and tilted her tear streaked face up to his. "Can you honestly say you don't want to be with me?"

She couldn't trust herself to answer.

His gaze wandered searchingly over her face. He leaned forward and kissed her gently on the lips. "I'm leaving Thursday."

Involuntarily her hand flew to her mouth. "Thursday?"

"Yes. Since Ross agreed to sell I've got to report back to my bosses to conclude the financial arrangements. I've finished my work here."

He smiled crookedly as though the thought had just come to him. "Come with me. I have to go to New York first then we'll go to Chicago. That's my town! I'll show you the city and buy you anything you want. We can travel anywhere in the world and do all the things you've most wanted to do." He hesitated. "Will you come with me?"

He watched knowingly as conflicting emotions flew across her face. Her eyes darted from his face to her home back to his face, down to her trembling hands and back to her home.

"I can't go. Everythin' that matters to me is right here. I can't go." But her expression gave the lie to her words.

"Whatever you say, Lu. But think about it. The train leaves at 3:30 a.m. You could slip out of town without having to explain to anyone." His eyes shone fervently.

"Think about it, Lu." He turned and walked away.

"You're feelin' a whole lot better this mornin', I see."

"Oh yes, ma. I'm all over whatever was wrong yesterday. How 'bout I run out and get those eggs in?"

After Lulabelle left Ila Rose thought about the difference in her daughter today. Whatever was ailin' her must be all cleared up now. That's good.

Yet, something didn't feel right. Something continued to nag deep within her. Lulabelle was chipper this morning, but it was a frenzied sort of chipper. Ila Rose had sensed the currents that swirled around Lulabelle. And yet there was nothing she could really put her finger on. *Maybe my suspicions were wrong after all,* she hoped, *maybe none of this has anything to do with Mr. Jones.* She hadn't seen him anywhere near Lu. Still, she felt uneasy.

"Well, Lu, I see you decided to join us common people agin."

"Bert!" She exclaimed merrily, "I never left you common people."

"Well you've sure kept yourself scarce the last while. Come and give your ole Bert a kiss."

Lu slipped around him. "Not now, Bert. I gotta get these eggs in to ma."

"That's never stopped you before. Come on, Lu, one little kiss ain't gonna slow you down none."

Lu ducked under his outstretched arms then turned, gave him a peck on the cheek and was on her way to the house before he could stop her.

Now that ain't like Lu, he thought. He watched, perplexed, as she shut the door behind her.

Ila Rose saw Bert sneak past the house a minute later. *Well, that's a relief,* she concluded, *it looks like Lu's back to her old tricks.*

When Jake and Neil came in Lulabelle seemed especially happy to see them. "I thought you'd never get here!" she exclaimed.

Surprised, Neil glanced at the clock. "This is the same time we get here every morning."

"I know. I'm just so darn glad to see you both." She hugged Jake until he squirmed, "Let go, ma. I can't breathe."

She smiled coquettishly at Neil and said, "What about you, big boy? Think I can squeeze the breath outta you?"

"Any time you want, Lu. Any time you want." They embraced for a long time. Then he placed his hands on her shoulders, took a deep breath and said reluctantly, "I've really got to go. I'll have to break the speed limit as it is to make it on time now."

Lulabelle watched him leave with such a tender, wistful look that Ila Rose was surprised. She knew Lu really did love Neil, but she'd always been so playful about it. She'd never gazed after him like that before. *Everythin' is okay,* she repeated to herself, *everythin' is okay. Then why don't I believe it?*

When Neil got home from work the table was set with their best dishes, a bouquet of colorful tulips resplendent in Lu's grandmother's crystal vase in the center.

"Whose birthday is it? Did I miss something?"

Lulabelle laughed. "No, you didn't miss nothin'. Can't a girl surprise her man once in awhile?" Her arms tightened around his waist as she lifted her lips to be kissed.

"Mama! When are we goin' to eat?" Jake grinned. Mama and daddy weren't like his friends' parents. They weren't embarrassed to show their affection. Still he liked to tease them about it.

Neil laughed. "Just wait till I wash my hands and comb my hair." He hurried from the room.

"It looks real nice, mama. Are we havin' a party?"

"Well yes, I guess you could say that."

"What's the party for?"

"Why, just for fun, Jake. Don't you think we ought to have a party just for fun sometimes?" She hugged him and tousled his hair.

"All right you two," Neil came in slicking down his wet hair, "time's a'wasting. Let's eat."

They'd had lots of high spirited suppers together but this one was extra special. Everything had turned out perfectly. *I'll never forget this night,* thought Lu as she carried a chocolate cake and set it carefully on the table while her two menfolks exclaimed over its beauty and rich aroma.

After Jake was in bed, Neil and Lulabelle once again sat on the front porch enjoying the fragrant air and full moon.

"What would you choose, Lu, if you could have anything in this world?"

Lulabelle didn't answer for a long time. Finally she touched Neil's cheek with her cool fingers and said, "I guess a girl shouldn't want more than I already got," she hesitated, "should she?" Her voice carried a note of melancholy. "Should she, Neil?"

"When Lu comes in will you tell her..."

"Lu? What are you talkin' about?" The look on Ila Rose's face was frightening.

Neil took a step toward her. "Are you all right?" He pulled a chair out from the table. "Here, Ila Rose, sit down." He helped her into the chair.

Her eyes were twitching wildly and her face was without color. He was afraid she might be having a stroke. "Should I get Doc Swenson?"

Ila Rose shook her head back and forth slowly. "No. No. I'm okay. I guess I'm just gettin' old." She took a deep, shuddering breath, "What was it you wanted me to tell Lu?"

Neil watched her compose herself. "It's nothing. Don't worry about it."

"Tell me," she demanded. "What is it you want her to know?" She held herself erect, willing her body to be strong and her voice clear.

"I just wanted to remind her that I'll be working a couple of hours extra today so I won't be home till about eight."

"Okay, I'll tell her. You go on, Neil. You'll be late. I'll tell her." She looked over to the table where Jake was eating his eggs and potatoes. She tried to smile at him. It came out a grimace, a horrible caricature of a smile.

"Are you sure you're all right, Ila Rose? It won't take a minute for me to get the doc."

"No. I'm okay. You go on. You'll be late for work. I'll just sit here for a minute and rest. Then I'll be fine. You go on."

She watched with growing alarm as he walked out the door. Lu? He thought Lu was here? Dear Lord, don't let that girl do what I'm afraid of. Let her be stoppin' somewhere to visit or flirt and just be late gettin' here. Let her walk in here now.

But Lulabelle didn't come. Ila Rose looked at the clock. "You better get on your way, Jake. It's soon time for school to start."

"Okay gramma. I'm leavin'. You sure you're okay? You look sick."

"I'm fine, Jake. Just a little tired. Hurry now. Get goin'. And come straight here after school today," she added.

He looked puzzled. "Here?"

"Yes. I got some things I need you to help me with so hurry here as soon as school's out."

He shrugged and nodded. "Okay." *Grownups sure are funny sometimes,* he thought as he went out the door and down the steps.

Ila Rose walked into the dining room. "Everythin' okay in here?"

The men nodded and began pushing back their chairs.

"If there's anythin' else you need, tell me now. I gotta go out for awhile." She turned to leave.

"Oh, Ila Rose," called Jack Beckman, "that city slicker didn't come down to breakfast yet. He might need somethin'."

"No, he left early this mornin'." She walked stiffly into the kitchen and out the back door, forcing her feet to take one step at a time. First I'll check Lu's place and see if she's gone back there. Then I know where I gotta go, she thought with dread.

Lulabelle wasn't in the house or anywhere outside. Ila Rose climbed the hill in back to see if she'd gone up there. She found the crest vacant just like she expected it would be. She climbed back down slowly, walked back into the house and looked in the little closet in the bedroom. She could see at a glance that some of Lu's clothes were missing.

She knew where she had to go now but she had to force herself in that direction. "Luke, were you workin' this mornin' when the Denver train left?"

"Yep." He turned to face her. "You look poorly, Ila Rose. You sick?"

"No, no, I'm fine," she said impatiently. "Did you see who got on the train?"

"There was only four people." He scratched his chin, "Bill and Emma Thompson, that Mr. Jones that's been staying at your place and, of course, Lu. She said she was goin' to visit Everett and his family over in Grand Junction for awhile." He continued, "I didn't know Everett was over there."

"Yes," Ila Rose lied, "they're livin' over there now." She turned to go, "Thanks, Luke, I just wanted to make sure Lu got off okay."

She hurried home. I was afraid of somethin' like this, she reflected. I kept tellin' myself she wouldn't get suckered by that scoundrel, but all along I was afraid of this very thing.

What'll I tell Neil and Jake? The rest of the town can think she's visitin' Everett for the time bein'. Jake might even believe it, though he'll be surprised she didn't tell him. But what am I goin' to say to Neil? He'll never believe a cocka-mamie story like that. No, I'll just have to tell him the truth. Poor man. It'll break his heart.

She walked into her kitchen and slammed the back door. "Damn that Butch Jones and damn that stupid, silly girl! Damn! Damn! Damn!"

* * *

May 29, 1934

Dear Neil,

Please don't throw this away till you read all of it. I know you must hate me. I can't explain why I did it. I don't know myself. I just know I had to. I'm writing this on the train out of Denver. I'd have sent a card before but that nosy-parker in the post office would've read it. I don't know what you told anybody. I told Luke at the station I was going to visit Everett in Denver. I guess I have to live with whatever you tell people. I don't deserve you to cover up for me but you and Jake deserve better than I'm doing to you. When I get a address I'll send it and hope you'll find it in your heart to write and tell me how you and Jake are. I'm writing the same thing to ma. I don't know if you can find it in your heart to forgive me. I know I haven't got a right to ask it. In spite of what I've done I do love you and Jake and always will. I wish I could've been satisfied.

Love, Lu

* * *

"Have you heard anything more from Lu since that letter three weeks ago?" Ila Rose heard the sadness in Neil's voice.

They were sitting at her table in the kitchen while Jake played with his stick horse in the back yard. A slight breeze blew the cool evening air in through the screen door.

"No. I haven't heard another word. I keep lookin' for a letter every day but nothin' comes." She paused, "Sometimes I wonder how much longer Jake will believe she's comin' back."

"He's got to keep believing," Neil said passionately. "We've got to believe she'll come home." He continued softly, "Maybe I'm a fool but deep in my heart I believe the time will come when the adventure she thought she was missing out on will wear thin and she'll be back."

"And what about you? Will you take her back after this?"

He looked thoughtfully at Ila Rose. "Oh yes. I love that girl. And I'm sure she loves me. I think she was blinded by slick words and a man completely different from anyone she's ever known before. Any one of us can make a mistake. I'm not giving up on her and I'm going to make sure Jake doesn't give up either. We'll both just keep on loving her."

"Has any of the kids said anythin' to him 'bout his ma?"

"So far people seem to believe she's with Everett. If she stays too long they might begin to wonder. I just hope Jake never learns the truth."

"You're a good man, Neil. Lulabelle don't deserve you. But I'm sure glad you're not bitter about her."

"I've always loved her. Maybe that was part of the trouble. Maybe I didn't give her enough time to get all this out of her system before we got married."

Ila Rose sighed and thought, *I just hope he's right and she does come to her senses and come back. She's not a bad person, just a weak one.* They sat in companionable silence, each wrapped up in what might have been and what could still be.

"Thanks for taking care of Jake while I'm at work, Ila Rose."

"You don't have to thank me. I'm glad to do it. He's a good boy and a help to me." She didn't add that his presence helped her get through the lonely, frustrating days since Lu had left.

Two weeks later, after Ila Rose had finished cleaning up the breakfast things and was mixing the bread dough, the phone in the hall rang. Even though it was the only phone in town it seldom rang, and even then it was usually in the late afternoon or evening.

Drat, who can be callin' at this time of the morning, she thought as she wiped her hands on her apron and hurried into the hall.

"This is the long distance operator. I have a reverse charges call from Lu Thomas. Will you accept the call?"

"Yes." Ila Rose looked carefully down the hall to make sure no one was around.

"Ma, is that you?" Lulabelle's voice was strained and quivering.

"Yes, it's me. Where are you? How are you?"

Lu's words came fast. "I'm in Chicago." She hesitated then hurried on, "Can I come home?"

"You? Alone?"

"Yes, ma, just me."

"Of course. When?"

"That's the problem. I haven't got any money and..." She began to cry.

"Don't worry about the money. I can rustle up enough to send you for a train ticket. Where do you want me to send it?"

"I don't know. I can't go back where I've been staying. I don't know what to do."

Ila Rose paused, trying to remember the layout of the Chicago train station when she and Eddie and their two little boys had passed through there all those years ago on their way to a new life in Utah.

"Is there still a telegraph office in the train station?"

Lulabelle thought hard, trying to remember what she had seen as they hurried through the station to the street outside. "Yes. I remember seein' it down at one end."

"How soon can you get there?"

"It'll take about a half hour to walk there."

"Go there and wait. I'll leave right now and go to the telegraph office in Bentwood. I can be there in a little over a half hour. I'll send the money to you there. Wait right there at the office till the money comes. Then buy a ticket on the next train headed this way." She added, "There'll be a little extra so you can get stuff to eat on the way."

"Oh, ma," Lulabelle sobbed, "I don't know how to thank you."

"Don't waste time on that now, Lu. Get to the station as fast as you can." Ila Rose hung up the phone and turned to see Jake standing in the kitchen doorway watching her.

"Is mama comin' home? Why are you cryin' gramma?"

She blew her nose. "I'm not cryin' I just got a stuffy nose." She put her arms around him so he couldn't see her face. "Come on, you can go for a ride with me." Then she took him by the hand and smiled, "Yes, your mama'll be home soon."

"I'm sure glad. Daddy's tried real hard to fix stuff I like for supper while mama's been gone, but I sure do miss her cookin'."

Ila Rose laughed. "I reckon your daddy's missed her

cookin', too." *And a whole lot of other things,* she thought. Well, he believed she'd come home and now she is. I hope his love for her is as strong as he thinks it is. He'll need a whole lot of tolerance to make up for what she's done.

"Is it true what Jake said? Is Lu coming home?" Neil stood just inside the kitchen door looking anxiously at Ila Rose.

"Yes, it's true. She oughta be here by the weekend."

Neil's smile was radiant. All Ila Rose's reservations about whether his love for Lulabelle was really strong enough to forgive her faded away. "The train from Denver comes in at ten o'clock at night. I wish I knew for sure which night she'll be on it."

"It doesn't matter," he said quietly. "I'll meet the train every night until she gets here."

* * *

"We're goin' to have a hard winter," Ila Rose said to Lu. "All the signs are pointin' in that direction." It was the first week in October and already the trees were bare and the nights were cold.

Ila Rose was proved right. By February the snow was fence top deep and blizzards continued to blow across town every few days. Jake and his friends thought it was great to sleigh ride and build snow forts but Lulabelle dreaded every step she took outside the house, fearful of falling on the slippery paths.

"I don't know if I can make it this time," she told Neil one cold night as they lay in bed listening to the wind whistle through the rafters. "I don't remember bein' this miserable last time."

Neil gently caressed her cheek. "You'll be fine, Lu. Don't worry. And rest as often as you need to. Jake and I can take care of things around here."

"You're so good, Neil." Her voice shook. "You've never asked me about my crazy spell."

"I didn't need to. You came back. That was enough for me."

Lulabelle whispered, "I couldn't talk about it before but I need to tell you now."

"If you really want to, Lu. But you don't have to explain anything."

"I'm not sure why I went. He seemed so smooth and so excitin'. And, even though I love you and Jake, I felt like I was missin' out on somethin' wonderful in life—somethin' that might never come again."

She sighed deeply. "It wasn't wonderful at all. He lied about everything. But even if he hadn't, I felt so cheap and dirty. Soon after we got to Chicago I wanted to come home. But I didn't have any money. I even asked him to loan me enough for a ticket home, but he laughed in my face. He said if I was so hot to go back I could figure out how to get there by myself."

Neil lovingly wiped away a tear rolling slowly down her face. "You don't need to go on."

"Yes. I do. I never saw him after that. The rent was paid in that crummy little boardin' house for the rest of the month. I stayed in the room there wonderin' what to do. I was too ashamed to call you. Then when the rent was due, the landlady told me to pay up or ship out. She said she didn't cotton to deadbeats.

"I realized then that was just what I was, a deadbeat. I left and walked till midnight. I tried to sneak in the lobbies of three hotels but they all kicked me out. I found a poor little church open and slept on one of the benches till mornin'. Then I walked some more till I got up enough courage to call ma."

She remained silent for a long time but Neil didn't say anything. He knew she wasn't finished.

Finally she said, "When I got off the train and saw you waitin' on the platform I was so ashamed I nearly climbed back on the train. Then you walked over and took me in your arms and I knew you'd forgiven me. I knew then that you and Jake and ma were all the excitement I'd ever want again. I realized then what love really is and how much I love you."

Neil kissed her and said, "I told you I'll always love you and always be here for you. Let's put all that behind us now and forget it ever happened. You're my wife and I love you. And you love me. That's all that really matters."

I'll make it up to him if it takes the rest of my life, thought Lulabelle. *The flirtin' and teasin' are ended. I'm through with that kind of life.* She fell asleep enveloped in a great and wondrous peace.

* * *

"Jake! Run and tell grandma to come quick!"

"What's the matter, mama?"

"Just run fast and get grandma. Tell her it's time and to come quick!"

Jake grabbed his coat and ran down the muddy road as fast as he could. He burst into the back door yelling, "Gramma! Gramma! You gotta come quick!"

Ila Rose looked up from the pot of soup she was stirring. "What's the matter, Jake?"

"Mama says to come right now! She says to tell you it's time!"

Ila Rose lifted the soup onto the back of the wood stove to keep warm. She glanced at the calendar as she slipped on her coat.

Dammit, she thought, *I hope Lu's not been lyin' to us. It wasn't supposed to be for another three weeks.*

As they hurried down the steps she said to Jake, "Run to Uncle Duane's and tell Aunt Lucinda I need her to come to your place as fast as she can. Then ask Uncle Duane to drive up to Swazie's ranch and tell your dad to come home."

"Come home? He said he'd be helpin' up there all day."

"Just do what I say, Jake. And hurry." When he ran out the front gate Ila Rose called, "And Jake, stay and play with your cousins till somebody comes for you."

Neil hurried up the steps and into the house. Lucinda smiled at him. "Go on in. Lu's waiting for you."

He pushed the bedroom door open quietly. Ila Rose got up from the rocker by the bed and walked over to him. "Everythin's okay. Go on over and sit."

She slipped from the room. Neil walked quickly over to the bed and smiled down at an exhausted Lulabelle, gazing tenderly at the baby in her arms.

"Come and see your little daughter, honey." She pulled the corner of the blanket away from the baby's face. "Isn't she the most beautiful baby you ever saw!"

Neil kissed Lulabelle gently on the forehead. "She is that, sweetheart. Have you decided what you want to name her?"

Lulabelle smiled. "Amelia Rose." She added softly, "Bein' named after both her good grandmas ought to give her the right start in life, don't you think?"

Neil nodded and smiled. There wasn't a doubt in his mind that she would, indeed, grow up to be like those two good women.

Chapter Five

Mirror Images

Saturday, August 10th, 11:20 a.m.

"Mama told me a lot about growing up in Creekston but I always had the feeling she was leaving something out. And she always talked about what a good man dad was." Amelia Rose smiled at the memory.

"She was sure right there. He was the salt of the earth."

"I've always thought so. I don't know if you remember but he died just six months after I got married."

"Yes. I remember that. I got the feeling at the time he was holding on, waiting till you were safely settled. He loved you very much, you know."

"I know he did. I can't remember him ever saying a cross word to me. Or to Jake, either, for that matter," she laughed, "and sometimes I thought he ought to get after him."

Duane laughed. "Oh yes, your brother did take after your mother. Every one of us thought that all the time he was growing up."

"That's true. Even mama used to laugh and talk about how much Jake was like her." She paused. "You know, just a day or so before dad died he took my hand and asked me to always take good care of mama." Tears came to her eyes. "He said he'd always loved her and that he'd be there to welcome her when she came back home to him again."

"He was a gentle and loving man. And you are just like him." He smiled, "In fact, you're the spitting image of him."

"I've always seen the resemblance in pictures of us together. But people tell me that all the time, too. It's the highest compliment I can think of."

Amelia Rose leaned over and kissed Duane. "It's been so good to visit with you. I'll come back again before we leave." She squeezed his hand then turned and walked toward her family.

"How are you feeling, dad?" Trailed by a handful of grandchildren shouting "Hi, Grandpa D," Melissa sat down by Duane, giving him a quick hug.

"I'm glad you all got here okay." Seeing the baskets and sacks they were carrying, he said, "Put your food right here on the table. There's plenty of room."

The children helped Melissa set their places then ran off to play with their cousins.

"Where's Bill?"

"He's over there talking to Jake and Barbara," she replied pointing to a table near the platform where the microphone stood.

Sitting down by Duane she said, "I hope we eat soon. We're starved."

"I suspect we'll start soon. You know how it is. Jess's family is in charge of the reunion this year so we can't eat until R.J. calls on somebody to give the blessing on the food. Can you see him?"

"He's getting the speakers hooked up to the mike. I hope that's a good sign," she laughed.

"You know," she said, "I've never even thought of it until now, but what does the R.J. stand for? That's all I've ever heard him called and I guess I just thought it was his name. Is it?"

"No. It stands for Ralph Jess. The Jess is for his dad, of

course, but the Ralph is for my brother Ralph who was killed in a plane crash three years before R.J. was born. Jess and Ralph were real close growing up and Ralph's death was awful hard on Jess."

Duane indicated to his right. "Look over there and tell me who that is."

"Which one?"

"That one in the green shirt."

Melissa looked closer. "I believe it's either Roy or Ray. I never could tell those two apart."

"You're not the only one. When they were growing up both of them were in constant hot water for filling in for one another when they were supposed to be doing their own work."

"I remember hearing some of those stories. Were they all true?"

"Nearly every one, I believe. They answered for each other at school and at church and even dated each other's girls without telling the girls."

"Wasn't their dad a twin, too?"

"Yes. Rudy and Rafe were so much alike they were like two sides of the same coin. They were so close they waited until they found sisters they both liked and married them on the same day."

A commotion erupted at the south end of the pavilion. "What's going on? What's happening?"

"I can't see from here. Hold on a minute and I'll check." Melissa was gone less than a minute. "It's Cousin Cora."

"Hell's bells, not again! What's she up to this time?"

"She's complaining that somebody usurped her table. That's the exact word she used—usurped."

"Well, if it isn't that it'd be something else as ridiculous."

"How'd Russell ever come to marry her? Was she always

like that?" She laughed. "And how'd we all get to calling her Cousin Cora when we don't call anyone else 'cousin'?"

"It started a long time ago, before we moved from Creekston. She grew up on a farm just outside town. Even when she was little she was different. Then, when she got in high school, she started chasing after the boys." Duane laughed. "To tell the truth, it was a two way street. They chased her, too."

Chapter Six

Russell

"Come on, Cora, it'll be fun."

She smiled coyly, looking at him with half closed eyes. "Well, Russ, I don't know. I might be busy."

"For crying out loud! That's why I'm asking this early."

She loved to tease him. Boys were so gullible. The Valentine's Day Dance wasn't for another month. They both knew it. They both knew, too, she could go to it with any boy in school. All she had to do was flutter her eyelashes and pull her mouth into that famous little moue and she could get anything she wanted. With her pert little nose, striking violet eyes and long blonde hair, none of the other girls could hold a candle to her.

"Oh Russ, you are so cute when you get mad." she sighed audibly, placed her finger softly on his lips and said, "Give me until tomorrow. I'll meet you right here at noon."

She loved stringing him along but knew she could push him only so far. Her most exciting challenge this year had been pushing him to the point of rejection then calling a halt before she'd crossed the line.

Cora did the same thing with all the boys, but Russell was the only one who wouldn't play the game to the end. And that was the very thing that made him more appealing than any of the others. She could never abide a pushover. Besides, Russell, with his flashing black eyes and dark wavy hair was the best looking boy in school.

After school he hurried to the store where he worked

from three to closing and all day Saturdays, stocking shelves and bagging groceries. He was glad to have the job. He'd worked at the store since ninth grade. With the money he earned, last summer he was able to buy, with a little help from dad, a used Ford coupe with a rumble seat.

He spent all summer and fall replacing nearly all the parts and painting it a beautiful two-tone green. He was the only boy in school with a car of his own, consequently all the boys in town hung around him every free minute. The girls coaxed for rides, too. They didn't have to worry about competing with Cora as she lived a few miles from Creekston and had to ride the bus home after school every day.

"I saw you smooching with Cora at school today, Russ," teased Naomi Rose as the family sat around the supper table.

Russell didn't answer. Naomi Rose was two years behind him in school and had dogged his steps every inch of the way. He knew not to get involved when she was trying to start something.

"Is that true, Russ? Were you and Cora smooching?" asked twelve-year-old Edward seriously. He thought the sun rose and set in his big brother and didn't want him to get into trouble.

Russ tousled Eddie's hair. "Naw, it's not true. You know Naomi Rose just likes to gossip."

"I do not, Russell Marsh! I did too see Cora Clark hanging all over you!"

Russ laughed but didn't respond. The best way to get to her was to ignore her. Nothing made Naomi Rose madder than being ignored. She was always poking her nose into someone else's business. But Russell knew her too well to feed into her games.

"You're dumber than you look, Mr. Bigshot, if you think

Cora's really interested in you. She can get any boy she wants just by snapping her fingers." She grinned impudently, "And everybody knows she makes out with every boy in town."

"Naomi Rose!" Naomi looked at her daughter angrily. "You will not use that kind of language in this house!"

"But mom..."

"No buts about it, young lady! You heard your mother!" Jess looked resolutely at her. "You will talk like a lady or you will go to your room! Now, apologize this minute."

Sulking, Naomi Rose mumbled, "Okay, okay. I'm sorry. But what I said is true."

"That's not the point. The point is you will watch your tongue and stop being such a busybody!"

Naomi Rose caught Russ's mocking glance. She ducked her head and finished her supper in silence.

In bed that night Russell thought about Cora and what Naomi Rose had said about her. He'd heard it before. But he didn't care. He wasn't going to marry the girl, he just liked taking her out.

Cora's reputation had grown more unconventional every year. Even in elementary school, she was different than the other girls. She could outrun, outcuss and outsmart any boy in school. She was the most determined competitor any of them had ever seen. None of the boys would let her play on their ball teams, afraid she'd beat them there, too.

In junior high school she changed her tactics from physical superiority to informational superiority. She knew more about cars, sports, occupations and anything else in the masculine domain than any boy in town and could spout statistics faster than anyone could challenge them.

By high school, she'd switched tactics again. Now she used her eyes, her lips, the flip of her hair over her shoulder and provocative body language to capture the hearts of all the boys. She led each one on mercilessly, giving him the impression he was the most important person in her life, then dropped him when she tired of her little games. But the games never deterred the boys. They still came back for more no matter how many times she rejected them.

Russell knew all this about her. They'd gone all through school together. Once in a great while he thought he glimpsed a vulnerability in her expression but it was so fleeting, even at the time, he wondered if he'd imagined it.

The Valentine's Dance was a huge success. Couples swirled around the floor in a rainbow of hues as full skirted dresses flared out over yards of ruffled net. The gym was decorated with red and white crepe paper streamers which swayed in the breeze created by the dancing couples.

"You look great tonight." Russell smiled at Cora in her lavender chiffon dress which emphasized her beautiful eyes. "Are you having fun?"

"You know I am," she replied as she snuggled closer, her breath warm on his neck. "I swear, Russ, you're the best dancer I know."

At midnight the orchestra leader announced the final medley. "I'm in the mood for love," Cora sang softly with the music, "simply because you're near me." Her eyes held promises of wonderful things to come.

She hummed as the music merged into Star Dust and Deep Purple. Then, once again, Cora gazed lovingly into Russ's eyes as she softly sang with the orchestra, "It must have been moonglow that led me straight to you."

His arms tightened around her as he found himself pulled into the magic of the night.

She was careful not to let Russ see her triumphant smile.

She knew she'd conquered again as they slipped on their coats and walked arm in arm out to Russ's car.

"Hi Russ." He adjusted the headgate and watched the water flow down the irrigation ditch. "Haven't seen you around much lately."

Russell smiled. "I've been pretty busy Uncle Duane."

"Let's see now, you graduate next month, don't you?"

"Yes."

"It sure doesn't seem possible. The time has gone so fast." There had always been a close bond between Duane and this special nephew.

Duane observed Russell more closely noticing the pinched look around his mouth and the dejected droop of his head.

"Something troubling you, Russ? You look kinda peaked."

"Aw, Uncle Duane, I hate to bother you," he paused, "but I don't know who else to talk to."

Duane put his arm around Russell's shoulder. "Come on. Let's go sit under that tree."

Russell hurried into his explanation as though afraid that if he didn't he'd lose his nerve. "Do you know Cora Clark?"

"You mean that pretty little thing I've seen with you sometimes?"

"Yeah," he answered bitterly, "me and every other boy in town." He hesitated not knowing quite how to go on.

Duane read his frustration. They'd been too close over the years for him to misunderstand. "Why don't you just tell me, Russ," he said quietly.

Russell hung his head. "She says we've got to get married. She says she's going to have a baby."

"Is it yours?"

"It could be." Then he added sarcastically, "Course it could be most any other boy's, too."

Duane was thoughtful. "Well, that is a problem. Let's see, you're only seventeen, aren't you?"

"Yes. I'll be eighteen in August."

"How old is Cora?"

"She's a couple of months younger than me."

"You're both awful young."

"I know." He added vehemently, "And awful stupid, too!"

Duane didn't say anything. There was nothing he could say that would alter the situation.

"It's more than just getting married."

"What is it?"

"I know this sounds stupid but we only made out once. Is it possible for a girl to get pregnant just one time?"

Duane swallowed his smile. "Yes," he said seriously. "It's possible. But why does she think the baby's yours?"

"I don't know. She just says she's sure."

"But you're not. Were you serious about her being intimate with other boys?"

"According to the boys, they've all slept with her."

"But surely you know that's how boys brag?"

"Yeah, I know. But some of 'em are right. Even Cora admitted that when I pressed her. But she still says she knows the baby's mine."

"I haven't heard anything here about love. Do you love each other?"

"I don't think either one of us knows what love is. I know I don't."

Duane squeezed Russell's shoulder. "Have you talked this over with your folks?"

"Not yet. I felt like if I talked to you first maybe I'd

come up with a solution." He waited. "Besides, you know how mom and dad are. They'll have a fit."

"Don't be too sure. I know they seem straight laced to you. Most parents seem like that to their kids. But I think you'll be surprised at their support if you talk to them."

"I know. I just hate to hurt them." He smiled ruefully, "It's a little late for that, isn't it?"

Duane didn't answer. He wasn't about to rub salt in Russell's wounds.

"Well, I gotta be going. Thanks for listening."

"Anytime, Russ. I think the world of you and know you'll make the right decision."

Russ turned back to face Duane. "Oh, I think I'd already made my decision before I came here. I just needed a good sounding board."

Russell and Cora were married the week after graduation. The ceremony was simple with only the two immediate families in attendance. The newlyweds went to Bentwood in Russ's car for a weekend honeymoon then moved into the little loft room over the store.

"I thought you said Cora was going to have a baby." Thirteen-year-old Belle was puzzled.

"She was going to have one. At least that's what everybody said." Naomi Rose was just as puzzled as her sister but trying not to show it.

"Well, here it is nearly Valentine's Day and she doesn't look one bit fatter."

Naomi Rose groaned. "I know. Maybe she had a miscarriage." She frowned, "But I haven't heard about it if she did."

"Russ looks kinda sickly, don't you think?"

"Yes I do." Naomi added, "He's not looked well all winter."

Jess asked worriedly, "You don't think there's anything the matter with him, do you?"

"He hasn't said anything to me. I've tried to ask him about it but he just says he's fine, everything's fine."

"Well, it sure doesn't seem fine," Jess said. "Has he or Cora ever said anything about losing the baby?"

Naomi sighed. "Not a word from either of them. I guess she must have lost it, though."

"There never was a baby, was there Cora?"

"Course there was, Russ. I told you I lost it." Cora grinned wickedly, "What's the matter? Don't you trust me?"

He looked at her in silence. No. He didn't trust her. And he didn't believe her any more, either. "When did you lose it?"

"I already told you," she replied angrily, "why do you keep harping on it?"

"If you're telling the truth then let's go over to Doc Harmer and find out why you lost it."

"Will you just drop it! I'm not going to go to that quack anymore. Now just forget it!"

He kept his eyes on her face. "You don't need to go. I already talked to him about it."

"You what?!"

"I went to him before Halloween when you were pretending you were pregnant but weren't showing any signs. I haven't said anything because I kept waiting for you to tell me the truth."

Her expression was livid. She opened her mouth to speak, then firmly snapped it shut again.

"He said you've never been to him. Not once. All the

time you said you were going for checkups, you were lying. You never were pregnant." His voice grew very low, "Why, Cora? Why do you keep lying about having a miscarriage? Why did you tell me we had to get married? Why did you tell me you were going to have a baby?"

With flashing eyes she hissed, "Why?! Because you were the best prospect I had for getting out of that house and into one of my own!"

Her voice rose, "My sanctimonious mom and dad thought I was just like my stupid sisters, that I liked going to church with them and being their 'good' girl.

"I finally got sick of it. I wanted to get away from the farm, to live in town, to do what I wanted without questions or lectures!

"So don't you start acting like you're my father! Don't start lecturing to me about truth and trust! I've had a bellyful of that kind of life!

"And if you don't like it," she grinned maliciously, "there's not a damn thing you can do about it. You married me for better or worse, for richer or poorer until death do us part.

"If you think you can change that, you've got another think coming! I like being married to the best looking boy in town with a car of his own and a steady job."

Cora leaned back in her chair and laughed harshly. "Just keep on bringing the money home dear Russ and I'll keep on being your sweet, dutiful wife, and everybody can just keep on thinking we lost our 'poor little baby' and feel sorry for us."

Russ got up, put on his coat and walked out the door, Cora's words echoing in his head as he walked heavily down the stairs and into the cold night. Cora heard the car start and listened with a smirk on her face as it rolled out of the yard.

Early in the morning two days later he came in, removed and hung his coat and sat down at the table. Cora watched him with questioning eyes but was determined not to give him the satisfaction of asking where he'd been.

After a long pause he said quietly, "Sit down, Cora. I've got something to tell you."

She sat, her composure shaken for the first time. He didn't seem like the Russ she knew.

"I've joined the Army Air Corps. I'll be leaving tomorrow."

"The Army Air Corps? What are you talking about? You can't just run off and join the Army Air Corps."

"I already did. I signed up yesterday in Bentwood."

"But you can't do that! What'll I do?"

He looked at her sadly. "I don't care what you do any more, Cora, but I'm sure you'll come up with something."

Her expression turned sly. "You think you can get me to divorce you by doing this, don't you?"

"No," he answered, his voice hollow, "I don't think anything. I just know I have to get away from you."

"Well, I can't stay here. I'll suffocate alone in this dumpy town. I'll follow you, Russ. I swear I will."

"You won't be able to. I'll go to a training camp first then, the way things are looking, I'll probably get sent overseas."

"How will I live?" she wailed. "What'll I do for money?"

"You'll get an allotment every month from my pay. I don't know whether it'll be enough for you to live the way you want or not. And frankly, I don't care." He smiled bitterly, "Maybe you'll even have to get a job."

"A job? Doing what?"

"I guess that's something you'll have to figure out."

"Why the Army Air Corps, son?" Jess couldn't hide his concern. "My brother Ralph was killed in a plane crash."

"I know, dad, and I'm sorry. But things are a lot different now than they were in 1917. Airplanes are a lot safer now."

"All the same," Naomi asked, "why join up?" She added hopefully, "Maybe we won't get involved in that war over in Europe."

"Well, if we do, mom, I'm of an age to get drafted right away. If I join now I can choose the service I want. That's why I signed up with the Army Air Corps."

He added reassuringly, "Don't worry. I'll be just fine. And this way I might even get to see some of the world." The smile didn't quite reach his eyes.

"But what about Cora, what will she do?"

"She's talking about moving to Bentwood and getting a job there. You don't need to worry about her. She knows how to take care of herself."

Jess tried to smile. "You're really set on this, aren't you? Well, may the Lord bless and watch over you."

In bed that night Naomi whispered, "There's more to it than just joining up before he gets drafted. I can feel it."

Jess felt it, too, but didn't want Naomi to stew over something they couldn't change. "Don't fuss. Everything'll be okay. That boy's got a good head on his shoulders. I'm sure he's thought this over carefully and is doing what he thinks is the right thing."

"I wish I could feel that."

"You worry too much, Naomi. Go to sleep. His train leaves early in the morning and we don't want him to go worried about us. Come on, mother, let's get some shut eye."

They didn't say another word that night. Nor did they get any sleep.

* * *

Russell's letters arrived regularly. Boot camp was tough but nothing he couldn't handle. The train ride to Fort Bliss was long and hot. Learning to fly was great but the army sure could've found a better place to teach aviators than out in the middle of the Texas desert. Rumors were circulating about their group being sent to Europe soon. Rumors were circulating about everybody getting a furlough soon. "Rumors are the lifeblood of the army."

"Mama! Mama! Russ's home!"

Naomi ran up the path from the garden where she had been picking tomatoes for supper. "Where is he, Johnny? Where is he?"

"Right here, mom." Out of the kitchen door walked Russell, taller, thinner and very tan.

"Oh Russ, it's so good to see you! We got your letter about coming and now you're really here!" She dropped the tomato basket and threw her arms around him. Stepping back to look at him again she said, "You look wonderful!"

He grinned, picked up the tomatoes and put them back into the basket and walked with Naomi and eleven-year-old John into the kitchen. "Is dad home?"

John spoke up, "Eddie ran to get him."

Just then Jess and Eddie rushed into the house. "Son, son, how good it is to see you!" Jess's voice quivered as he embraced Russell.

Russ returned the hug, patting Jess on the back all the while. Then he turned and swept Eddie and John into his arms. "Hi, you guys. Boy have I missed you!" He ruffled their hair and hugged them again." Where are the girls?"

"They'll be here soon. They had band practice. They'll be marching in the Fourth of July parade in Bentwood." Naomi's voice was filled with pride.

As the family sat around the supper table they talked of all the things that had happened in Creekston since Russ left. He seemed interested in every detail.

Later, after the rest of the family had gone to bed, Jess and Naomi and Russ talked late into the night. "Army life is about like I've written. There are more and more guys coming in every day. Barracks are being built as fast as possible, but they're still not keeping up with the demand. The weather's hotter than anything you can imagine and the wind blows dust everywhere all the time."

"What do your instructors think about the situation with Germany?"

"They think we'll be over there in full force before the year is out. England keeps asking for our help. We've already got men and planes in England but it looks like the U.S. will be in this war soon."

Jess spoke softly, "Yes, that's the feeling we get from what we read in the papers. I don't know if R.J. said anything to you but he and Mary are sure worried about him getting drafted if we go to war." He added, "Quite a few boys from the county are signing up now rather than wait for the draft."

"The Jensen boys and Tom Richards joined the Navy. The Reynolds boy from the farm up by the Clarks has gone to the Army Air Corps and Perry and Don Tibbets have joined the Marines. You went to school with most of them, didn't you?"

Russell looked at Naomi. Her face was more strained than it had been before he left. "Yes. A couple of them were ahead of me. And Don was a year behind. He must have graduated in May, didn't he?"

She nodded. "Some of the boys around here are talking of not going back to school in September but joining up now. Their folks are sure worried."

"They're nuts if they do. Service life isn't easy and there's no sense rushing into it."

"Are you sorry you joined when you did?"

"No. I was already out of school. And I'm getting some good flight training. But I wouldn't recommend anybody leaving school to join up early."

"We hear Cora's moved to Salt Lake. Will you get to see her?"

"No. I have to leave day after tomorrow so I won't be able to get up there."

"How are things between you two?" Jess looked troubled.

Russ answered calmly, "They're just the same. Everything's fine."

"Mrs. Clark said Cora's working in a store called Auerbachs and that she likes living in Salt Lake." Naomi kept her eyes down so Russell wouldn't see the concern in them.

"She always wanted to get out of Creekston." Russ laughed easily, "A big city like Salt Lake is a lot more her style."

"What about when you come home? Will you move up there or will you two come back here?"

Russ laughed again. "It's way too soon to worry about that now. We'll figure something out when the time comes."

"Russ, everybody in town has been asking about you." Naomi went on hesitantly, "You don't mind about the get together tomorrow afternoon, do you? I just couldn't disappoint all of them."

"No, I'm glad about it. It'll give me a chance to see everybody at once."

"That's good," Jess smiled, "Everett's girls and your cousin Beth Ann are bringing the food. They insisted. Said your mom should be free to visit you without worrying about things other people can do."

"That's mighty nice of them."

"You haven't said where you'll go from here." Jess didn't need to add there had hardly been a chance to get a word in. "Will it be back to Texas?"

"No. Our whole squadron is re-assigned to New Jersey. That's why there's so little time home. The train ride across the country will eat up most of our leave."

"How long will you be there?"

"I don't know. We've all heard rumors about being stationed there permanently and other rumors about being sent right to England from there. Only those in charge know for sure." He laughed, "And most of the time I wonder about them."

The train was crowded with other young servicemen heading east. The steady beat of the wheels lulled Russ into somnolence. His mind returned again to the last night he'd spent with Cora.

"Children?" There was no humor in her laugh. "Don't be ridiculous! I have no intention of having stretch marks and sagging breasts and all the rest that comes with that overrated state called motherhood—not to mention getting up in the night to feed a cranky kid. No, you can forget about that....

"Don't be stupid. Why would I want a divorce? I'll have the best of both worlds and still never have to wash any man's socks. You'll live your life and I'll live mine...

"Oh grow up, Russ," she'd taunted, "it's not the end of the world. Go ahead and play soldier boy but don't expect me to sit home pining away. I'm going where I can have fun, where there's life and excitement...

"No sense worrying about what happens when you come

home again. We'll go right on pretending to be the happiest couple around."

The words echoed in his head until they finally became one with the rhythm of the wheels and he slept.

* * *

Two days before Thanksgiving the letter they'd all dreaded arrived. Russ would be deporting the next day. Rumors flew like wildfire but his best guess was they would head for England.

The children thought it sounded like a great adventure but Jess and Naomi worried and prayed, having heard the stories of ships in the Atlantic being sunk by the German Navy. The word 'Thanksgiving' took on new meaning for the family as they joined together for dinner.

The next two weeks passed without a word from Russ. Then Sunday, December 7th, news came over the radio of the Japanese attack on Pearl Harbor.

"What does it mean, daddy?" Eddie's voice shook.

Jess looked at Naomi. "It means war has come."

"Here in Creekston?" Johnny had visions of planes flying overhead dropping bombs on them like he'd seen in the newsreels at the showhouse.

"No," Jess said quietly, "it means all our young men will have to go halfway around the world and fight so the war won't come here."

The Christmas festivities were quieter, more grave than usual. Even the children were subdued. And though everyone went to the New Year's Eve Dance, 1942 came in with anxiety rather than jubilation. Those who remembered The Great War knew with surety this would be the last time some of their young people would be here like this.

"Maybe it'll be over by next year," Naomi said hopefully. Jess hugged her for a long time. Words of solace wouldn't come.

The second week in January Jess hurried home from the post office with a letter from Russ. He'd written it the end of November.

He wrote that what he'd seen of the English countryside was beautiful, the people were friendly in spite of the hardships and shortages they were experiencing and that the morale of his fellow airmen was high. "With our arrival here it looks like this war won't last long at all."

They'd been told their mail would be censored. If there was anything in any letters that might be useful to the enemy it would be cut or blacked out so if he didn't give details they would understand why.

"This is my mailing address. I hope to hear from you soon although we've been told not to expect mail for some time. I'll write as often as I can but the letters will probably take quite awhile to get home. Don't worry about me. I'm fine and enjoying myself. There's a small Branch of the Church that meets in the upstairs room over a bakery just a few miles away. There are quite a few Mormons in our squadron so we meet with the Branch whenever we can. There are only about twenty local members so our guys nearly double the congregation when we're all there. I'm getting the hang of the local dialect and starting to feel right at home."

* * *

"So, Lieutenant, are you coming to our New Year's Eve dance?"

Russell smiled, "Will it be here?"

"Yes," she answered, "we'll just push the chairs back against the walls. Three of your lot are teaming up with our three musicians so we should have some smashing tunes. Will you be here?"

"I sure hope so. I'm not scheduled for duty that night so if nothing comes up I'll be here."

The music was lively and the crowd was in high spirits. Many of the Branch members had brought friends. Most of the local young men were away fighting so the U.S. servicemen were a welcome addition.

"Are you having a good time?" Moira's dark hair was cut in a bob that framed her elfin face. She had the beautiful alabaster complexion that was typical of so many of her countrywomen. The only makeup she wore was a touch of pink lipstick. Her green eyes glowed with pleasure as they danced.

"Yes. I'm having a great time. What about you?"

She nodded and smiled and almost forgot for awhile the reality of her world turned upside down.

When the last notes of 'Hail Britannia' faded away, everyone pitched in to help put the room in order. They worked comfortably together. There had been talk of animosity toward the Americans in some parts of the country but there was none in evidence here this night.

"A penny for your thoughts."

"I was just thinking how nice you've all been to us here."

"Well why shouldn't we be?" Her eyes flashed, "You're over here to help us!"

She shook her head. "I've heard some of the things that have been said. And I have met some pushy Yanks," she grinned, "but if you haven't already, you will meet some pushy Brits. That seems to be the nature of the beast. In spite of that I'm happy you've come. It appears we won't be out of this mess any too soon."

Russell agreed and added, "Most of our group won't be to church next Sunday. We're shipping out day after tomorrow."

A shadow flickered across her face. She knew that meant they'd be heading for the thick of things. She forced a smile and said, "I won't be here much longer either. I'm heading for London soon. They need ambulance drivers and I'm qualified."

She shook his hand, "Good luck, God bless, and may you return safely."

* * *

Russell gazed at the inhospitable landscape beneath them. Surely no living thing could long survive in such desolation. There to the west yawned the great Qattara Depression. It was more bleak and barren than the human mind could fathom.

And there ahead lay miles and miles of sand dotted with every kind of military vehicle. Some had been burned, some blown up and some simply abandoned as their passengers scurried for cover. British, German and Italian emblems were displayed randomly among the debris, evidence of violent fighting and rapid retreats.

If there is, indeed, a hell, Russ thought, *it must look exactly like this.* He glanced at the other members of his crew. His thoughts were mirrored in their eyes.

"It looks," one of the men muttered, "as though Rommel and his Afrika Korps have passed this way."

* * *

"Good to see you." Everett and Jess shook hands. "Reunion won't be quite the same this year with so many of our boys gone."

Jess nodded. "What do you hear from Ed?"

Worry lining his face, Everett answered, "He's just been sent to Fort Ord in California. We're all afraid that means he's on his way to the Pacific. Georgia and the kids have moved in with us for the time being. What about your boys?"

"We're not sure where Russ is. His mail still goes to England but his letters sound like he's off somewhere else. And R.J.'s still at Fort Bragg in North Carolina. He doesn't know where he'll go next. Mary and little Ralphie are over there talking to Ann and Phil and Beth Ann." He pointed to the people seated on a blanket under a tree.

Eddie and John were playing touch football with Charlie, Sam and Ev when a dark blue Ford pulled into an empty space at the edge of the park.

"Wowie! Who's that?" The game stopped as they all stared at the woman climbing out of the driver's side. They watched as she shut the door and turned toward them, a small basket in her hand.

Johnny looked questioningly at Eddie. "I didn't know she was coming."

"Neither did I," answered Eddie grimly. "I wonder what she's doing here."

"She can do anything she wants," exclaimed Sam giving a low whistle.

"Right on," added Ev, "she looks like a movie star." He grinned, "Let's go see if she needs us to carry anything."

They dashed toward the car. Cora watched them with a dazzling smile. She was well familiar with her power over the opposite sex. Even city males were no different than these small town yokels.

"Hi Cora," said Eddie gravely. "Want us to carry your stuff?"

"Well, if it isn't Eddie." She looked at him appraisingly then turned to the younger boy, "And this must be Johnny. You've both grown a lot since the last time I saw you."

She turned to the other three teenagers. "And who are these handsome gents?" Their faces reddened with pleasure.

"This is Sam and that's Charlie in the middle. They're both Ila Mae's boys."

"Let's see now. She's Everett's girl, isn't she?" Cora dimpled sweetly as she asked.

"Yes," his smile broadened in surprise that she remembered, "and this here's Ev."

"Yes. Bea's boy." She touched his cheek, "I know your daddy."

The boys were fascinated by her charm and beauty. They stood speechless, staring in awe. Then Charlie broke the ice, "You're Russ's wife, aren't you?" She nodded. "Did you come all the way down from Salt Lake?"

She nodded again and said, "Yes. I got off work this year specially so I could come to the reunion. I haven't been here for a couple of years and I figured it was time I joined the family this year." They were too enthralled to notice the wicked gleam in her eyes.

"Well, we're sure glad you came!" Sam grinned, gaping at the halo of curls framing her face. "Shall we call you Angel?"

She laughed along with the boys. "No honey, you don't need to do that. Cousin Cora will be just fine."

"Why do you think Cora came today?" asked Naomi Rose as the family prepared for bed.

"Why, she's part of the family. She should be here,"

answered Naomi stoutly, trying not to show her own hidden doubts.

Jess was puzzled also but kept his skepticism to himself. "She came because she's Russ's wife and she belongs here." He turned toward the bedroom, "Now let's go to bed. She came. We had a nice visit. And that's the end of it."

In bed later Johnny whispered, "Do you like Cousin Cora?"

Eddie laughed. "She's not our cousin."

"But that's what she said to call her."

"Yeah. Well, I guess that's as good as anything." He didn't add that he wasn't entirely positive but he had a faint memory of Russ looking sad when Cora's name was mentioned. So no, he didn't think he did like Cousin Cora very much.

"So how was that family reunion?"

Cora laughed, "It was just like I expected it to be. The old people are still boring, the only ones left around my age are the females and I never did like any of them, and the kids did nothing but gawk at their angelic Cousin Cora." She snuggled closer in his arms.

"Then why did you bother to go?"

"I don't know. Just curiosity, I guess."

And a lot of showing off, I suspect. "Was the trip worth using up all your gas coupons for the month?"

"Not really." She nibbled his ear. "Now can we get back to the business at hand and stop all this chatter."

"Of course," he replied fingering the top button of her blouse. "Have I ever told you how stunning you look?"

"Not nearly often enough." She sighed with contentment. *Even after everything that's happened I still have the ability to keep them eating out of my hand.*

* * *

The desert continued to serve as the focal point of the battle for supremacy in North Africa. Air and ground forces raged continuously. Russell and his B17 crew flew hour after hour, day after day.

Using tanks, field guns, tracked artillery and foot soldiers, Rommel's Afrika Korps swung south through Msus then east planting minefields along this front all the way to Bir Hacheim. It looked like he would be in Cairo before Thanksgiving.

Then the British Eighth Army met the Afrika Korps head on at El' Alamein. They took the offensive and rolled on to Tripoli and southern Tunisia constituting a major turning point in the war. The tide had turned. Great Britain was turning defeat into victory.

Their furlough in England was a welcome respite. "What're your plans, Russ?"

"I'm off to Salisbury for four days first. I didn't get out to Stonehenge last time. I'm determined to see it this time. What about you? What are you planning?"

Richard smiled tiredly, "I just want to stay right here in London and sleep for at least forty-eight hours. After that I'll decide how much sight-seeing to do."

"Where are you staying here?"

"I had a buddy who came in a couple of weeks ago reserve me a room at the Sandringham for these two weeks. When you get back look me up."

The train ride through Salisbury Plain was beautiful. The weather was balmy and the late fall colors were magnificent. Russell watched in amazement as the soaring spire of Salisbury Cathedral grew taller as the train approached.

The Cathredal had been impressive on his first visit but the sight of it now was more stirring. *Maybe,* he thought, *it's because I've seen how fleeting life is and how quickly it can be snuffed out.* His war-weary eyes took in the beauty around him with renewed appreciation for the wonder of life.

"Lieutenant Marsh! Is it really you?"

Russell turned with a start to see a familiar figure step out of the greengrocers. "Moira! How nice to see you again! I thought you were in London driving ambulances."

"I'm just home on leave for a few days. But what are you doing here?"

He smiled. "We've got a two week furlough and I'm hoping to recapture the sense of sanity I feared I'd lost out in the desert." He was very thin and looked very tired.

"Where are you staying?"

"I thought I'd try to get a room at an inn here."

"Come home with me, instead. Mum and dad will be glad to see you again. And Rob's room is there just sitting empty."

"Where is Rob now? Do you know?"

"The last we heard his group was being posted to the Irish Sea. Boche U-boats are stirring up trouble all along the west coast. We've not had any post from him since the first of October but we're keeping our prayers going. We can only hope that no news is good news."

Russell hefted his duffel bag onto his shoulder and they set off for the Dalrymple home at the east end of town. As they walked they talked of the war and their actions since the New Year's Eve dance. Although Salisbury was seeing its share of bombing, there was still a sense of continuity and life here. The futility of war seemed more remote now.

The Dalrymples were delighted to see Russ again and made his stay as pleasant as they could. They made it clear they were happy to have him stay in Robert's room.

Moira had to be back in London at the same time Russell

planned to return so next morning Amos, Maggie, Moira and Russell set out on bikes for an overnight trek to Stonehenge. As they pedaled along Russ felt the muscles in his legs expand and his lungs fill with clean, fresh air.

"This is wonderful," he panted as they pulled up the last rise. There before them rose the great stone circle which had been an enigma for centuries. They parked their bikes and walked slowly toward the monolithic circle before them.

"You see in the center," Amos explained, "there are two kinds of stones, sarsen and bluestones, so-called because of their color."

He read aloud from the guidebook, "All the sarsens have been carefully shaped by pounding their surfaces with heavy lumps of stone which gradually smoothed away the natural roughness. This stone is so hard that even with modern steel tools it is very difficult to cut. The shaping must have been done when the stones were still lying on the ground and could be rolled over with levers. When they were put upright, the stone hammers were wedged into the holes around their bases to hold them tight."

Russ marveled as Maggie added, "No one knows what Stonehenge was used for because there were no written records when it was built. Some believe it was used as a place of worship over a very long period of time. Others think it was a sort of observatory for recording the risings and settings of the sun and moon and to predict the eclipses of the moon. Neither theory can be proven."

Moira said quietly, "No matter how many times I see this place I am astounded and awed by its majesty."

"Yes," Russ agreed. "How mother and dad would enjoy seeing this. Some day, when this war is over, I want to bring them here."

"Can you say where your next posting will be?" Moira asked as the train carried them toward London.

"I'll be stationed at an air base here in England for the time being. We'll be chasing U-boats as well as bombing raids across the channel." Russell looked at her solemnly. "Tell me about your work."

Moira tried for lightness but fell short. "We're busy every minute. At first the Luftwaffe flew only during daylight hours. Our R.A.F. was outnumbered but had better planes and pilots and forced the Germans to give up daylight bombing. So they turned to night raids. For eight months they bombed us every night. It was terrible. Then our lot got better at tracking them..."

"Radar?" he interrupted.

She nodded. "They still get through but not in such numbers. You'll see. Air raids go on incessantly over London but we're getting right clever at driving around and through the rubble to get the injured to hospital."

She added quietly, "The hardest is when it's children. They live in fear every day yet try to be so brave. My heart just goes out to them."

He nodded. This terrible war had already gone on too long. But it wouldn't be over soon they both knew.

Their conversation turned to pleasanter things. Moira told of growing up with Robert and how close they'd always been.

Russell talked fondly about his family. He didn't mention Cora. They all knew he was married, he'd never tried to hide that. But he'd never said a word about his wife.

Moira thought it must not be a happy marriage. She had met other men who couldn't wait to pull photos out of their wallets and talk about their wives. She'd never seen Russ do that. Nor would she ask him to.

As they left the station and walked outside toward the steps of the underground trains Russell asked, "Where do you live here?"

"I've got a flat with three other girls in a mews off Hereford Road. What about you? Where will you be for the rest of your stay here?"

"I'll check in with Richard at the Sandringham. He said he'd try to get me a room there."

"Smashing! That's not too far from my flat. I know London very well now. Give me a ring," she wrote her telephone number on a slip of paper and handed it to him, "if you want a guided tour of London. There should be someone at the flat all the time. We work in shifts. If I'm not there, I'll get the message and get back to you."

"So how was Stonehenge?"

Russell smiled at Richard as they sat on a bench in Hyde Park and ate their fish and chips. "It was great. Even better than I expected. You ought to see it while we're here."

"I just might do that. Did you have any trouble getting a place to stay in Salisbury?"

"No. I ran into Moira, you remember the Dalrymples don't you?" Richard nodded. "Well, I stayed with them."

Suddenly the sirens sounded and rose in volume until they filled the evening air with their cacophony. Richard and Russell dropped their greasy newspapers in the garbage can as they vaulted toward the stairs of the nearest underground station to wait out the air raid.

Moira was as good as her word. she took them to see St. Paul's Cathedral, London Bridge, Covent Gardens, The British Museum, the Houses of Parliament, Tower of London, Royal Albert Hall and Buckingham Palace.

Sometimes it was just the three of them and other times additional friends joined them.

The final days of their furlough were rapidly coming to an end. They decided to pool their resources and have dinner at the Oxford Grille the night before Russell and Richard were to leave. When they arrived at the restaurant, they found a distraught Moira waiting for them.

She told them of the phone call from home she'd received earlier. "It's Rob!" she sobbed. "The filthy Huns have sunk his ship! That bloody Hitler! I hope he rots in hell!"

Russell took her in his arms and held her tight knowing that no words would comfort her just now. Richard hit his fist into the palm of his other hand and said, "Damn! Damn! Damn! You'd think we'd get used to this," his voice broke, "but we never do."

The three turned away from the restaurant and walked slowly toward Moira's flat. Then the sirens clamored to life. She turned to face them and, wiping her eyes, said shakily, "I'm needed. I can't bring Rob back but perhaps if we save other lives that will help make up for his sacrifice." She hugged them both then turned and hurried toward her post.

May 28, 1943

Dear Family,

I guess you've heard by now that the fighting in Africa is pretty well finished. I think I can tell you now without being censored that I was there the better part of last year. I thought the Texas desert was bad, but I didn't know what bad was until we got to North Africa.

We're flying raids out of England now. I don't know how long that will last.

I told you about the family I stayed with when I visited Stonehenge and that their son was killed in the Irish Sea. Well, last month the Dalrymples and their daughter invited me to meet them in York and stay with relatives there for a couple of days. I had time off then so went. York has a wall around the old part and a group of narrow streets called 'The Shambles' where there are all kinds of little shops. You'd love it mom. I hope to bring you all here after the war and show you around this beautiful country.

I've been in London a couple of times. Moira (Dalrymple) drives an ambulance there and takes us sightseeing when she has time off. She's a nice girl. You'd like her.

Wish I could describe the countryside we fly over but that would never get past the censor so you'll just have to wait until I get home.

I hope you are all fine and not worrying about me. I'm fine. I get to church services when I can. Hugh B. Brown was here not long ago and we had a wonderful meeting. There were over 70 servicemen there.

Your letters are getting to me pretty fast. I'm glad Naomi Rose is going to B.Y.U. Maybe I'll go there, too, when this war is finally over.

Love, Russ

* * *

"Thanks for coming, Russ."

"I'm sorry I didn't get back in time for the funeral." Russell looked at Moira sadly, "How are you holding up?"

She sighed, "I'm all cried out. Now there's nothing but this appalling emptiness." She paused, "And the irony of it is we anticipate the bombs, but to have a bloody drunk driver crashing into mum and dad just doesn't make any sense, somehow."

Russell hugged her and asked, "What will you do now?"

"I've told the agent to sell the house and most of the furnishings. I could never go back there and live. Too many memories. Oh, we had such wonderful times together." Her voice broke, "Damn and blast! I thought I'd shed enough tears to last the rest of my life."

"Will you stay here in London, then?"

"For now. I'll keep on with my work here. It's where I'm most needed." She looked up into his face, "And what about you?"

"I've got leave for a week. Word is we'll be flying out soon. With Sicily now in Allied hands, I think our squadron will be transferred there so we can help the push up through Italy." He smiled bleakly. "I've got a room at the Sandringham again for this week."

"Will I see you?"

"I want that very much. But I don't want to intrude on your plans."

She laughed softly, "Oh please intrude, Russ. I'd like for us to be together."

"Yes. So would I."

The week flew. They explored quiet, out of the way sections of the city and picnicked every day in a different park.

"You know," he commented as they walked slowly through Regent's Park admiring the rose gardens, "here one would never know we were in the middle of a war."

"Well," she smiled, "we British love our roses and not even Hitler's bombs can keep us from them."

It was the same as they walked through Hyde Park, Kensington Gardens and Green Park. Only in the parks was there a sense of serenity and continuation. In London proper it was impossible to walk very far without coming upon rubble from the repeated bombings. But in the parks, with their towering trees and carefully landscaped grounds, peace and solace calmed and surrounded them.

They spent every possible minute together. When the sirens blared, Russ ran with Moira to her post. While she helped load the injured into the ambulance and sped to the nearest hospital, Russ helped hunt for survivors and clear out debris. Neither of them had ever known such happiness and fulfillment.

Too soon the week was gone. Russell held Moira in his arms for a long time. They didn't notice the jostling as people hurried past entering and exiting the trains.

"Come back to me," Moira whispered.

"I will, my dearest, I will." He hopped onto the slowly moving train and they watched each other steadily as it pulled slowly out of the station.

Twining's Fifteenth Air Force flew sortie after sortie over Italy as the Axis forces were pushed slowly back. The Italian countryside became familiar to Russell and his crew as they flew day after day pin-pointing their targets with precision.

One day, Russ thought, *I want to come back here and see this country at peace.* The beautiful blue of the Mediterranean Sea combined with red tiled roofs and what was left of green foliage showing the promise of the inherent beauty Italy possessed.

* * *

16 April 1944
Dear Diary,

Have been listening to BBC. The news of the Allied bombing around Cassino sounds ominous. Wonder if Russ is there. He must be. How I pray for his safety. And not just for my sake anymore. Have been blessed with good health. Am still driving ambulance and will continue to do so as long as possible.

Have received some letters from Russ—the last one dated March 20th. He said the ground fighting has been horrendous. He didn't say where but I've been following the map as I listen to news broadcasts and am sure he must be talking about Anzio.

The girls are so good to me. They tell me they've worked out a schedule that will make it possible for one of them to be here all the time. They even volunteered to help with the 2 a.m. feedings. They're great chums. Couldn't ask for better.

Time for bed. Goodnight—and God bless Russ wherever he is.

* * *

Russell took his packet of letters and walked to a nearby stone fence to sit and read them. He arranged them in chronological order according to postage dates and began to read:

Everybody sends their love. Dad's chest pains have slowed him down some but he wants Russ to know he's okay now and can still haul hay faster than Eddie or John. (Not so, [Russ recognized Eddie's handwriting in the margin] but don't tell dad I wrote this.) . . . Naomi Rose has met Mr. Wonderful at B.Y.U. He's one of the Army Specialized Training cadets quartered on campus. They're planning marriage before he's called to active duty. . . . Eddie is taller than dad now and John isn't far behind. They're both in the school band. . . . Mom is fine—a little trouble now and then with numbness and blurred vision—but it's probably just old age so can't expect it to change. . . . Only a few young men left in town now. R.J. has been shipped to the Pacific. Mary and little Ralphie are holding up bravely. . . . You're in our prayers constantly.

Finishing their last letter, Russell paused and reminisced about his family. How he missed them! And how he missed the unaffected goodness of his childhood home. It would be good to see them again. *And somehow,* he thought, *I'm going to convince Cora to agree to a divorce so I can marry the woman I truly love.*

Uncle Duane's letters filled in the necessary details about Jess and Naomi. They both had health problems but the doctor said they were doing as well as can be expected and not to worry about them. Duane and Lucinda checked on them every day and helped out whenever they were needed. . . . Their own children were growing up too fast. They hoped the war would be over before David and Peter were old enough for the draft. . . They were still coping with the loss of their baby. "The poor little thing just didn't have the strength to live. But we're thankful for the Savior's atonement and know we'll see little Russ again." Lucinda still hoped for at least one more baby but the doctor wasn't very encouraging.

So they'd named the baby after him. Uncle Duane had told him if they ever had another boy that's what they'd do. Too bad the little guy didn't make it.

Then he opened the remaining letter. He'd saved it for last.

17 May 1944

My Dearest Russ,
      You'd better sit down. I've got a surprise for you. Or perhaps I should say we've got a surprise for you. You

see, I'm holding your beautiful little son on my lap as I write. He was born yesterday here in the flat as he couldn't wait for me to get us to hospital. But the doctor came and took great care of both of us. The girls have oohed and aahed over him continuously. Doctor says to stay home for a month then I'll be fine to go back to my post.

You told me to choose the name so I hope you'll agree with my choice. His name is Robert Jay after my dear, dear brother. I thought about naming him Russell but decided we'd wait and do that together with our next son.

I pray for you night and day. BBC gives an account each day of the fighting and I can imagine how it must be for you. It sounds as though our forces are closing in on Rome. There's a heightened feeling of anticipation here lately and so much activity along with it that we wonder.

Give your friend Richard my love and come back to us safely.

I love you, Moira

* * *

"Quick! Turn on the radio!" The news was astounding! Allied troops had invaded the Normandy coast beginning at 6:30 a.m. June 6th. They were calling it D-Day.

"General Eisenhower, the supreme commander of the Allied Expeditionary Forces," the announcer continued, "was reported to have told his forces they were about to embark on a great crusade. A naval task force carried troops across the English Channel. They landed on Utah, Omaha, Gold, Juno and Sword Beaches on the French coast. We've just received word that almost three million British, Canadian and American servicemen are in this vanguard."

Those gathered around the radio sat in silence. Then four-year-old Ralph asked, "Does that mean daddy will come home now, mama?"

Mary looked at Jess and Naomi. "Not yet, sweetheart. But soon." She lowered her head as they all prayed soundlessly.

* * *

The beleaguered population of London faced a new horror; Hitler's secret weapon, the vengeance bomb.

"It's really a guided missile, or a bomb that flies by itself. That's what makes it so terrifying. It's simply targeted in our direction then falls to earth and explodes when the power is gone."

Moira was aghast. "You mean to say no one is piloting the thing?"

"That's right," Sydney answered. "Their people just send it up and it flies over here and drops anywhere."

"But that's monstrous! I can understand the military trying to hit strategic targets but I can't begin to conceive of a weapon of such destruction aimed at civilians."

"Well, that's what those explosions were we heard last night. And they say from now on it won't matter whether it's day or night. Since there's no plane to shoot at, our lot will have a much harder time tracking them."

Moira returned to her post two days later. The damage from the VI bombs was random with no pattern at all to their impact.

As the days passed everyone grew to dread the sound of them. They were not heard until they were overhead. By then there was no time to seek protective cover. The most frightening moments came when the shriek changed to silence as the power was depleted and the hearer knew the bomb was plunging to the earth.

Now, even silence carried wicked foreboding to a people

already burdened with the hardships of siege.

"Sleep my little one," crooned Moira as she tried to dispel her own tensions before they spread to the baby. Then, into her mind came the words by Tennyson her mother had sung to her as a child. The words of the lullaby held new meaning for her now. Softly she sang:

"Sweet and low, sweet and low, wind of the western sea;
Low, low, breathe and blow, wind of the western sea;
Over the rolling waters go, come from the dying moon
    and blow,
Blow him again to me, while my little one,
while my pretty one sleeps.
"Sleep and rest, sleep and rest, father will come to thee
    soon;
Rest, rest, on mother's breast, father will come to thee
    soon;
Father will come to his babe in the nest,
silver sails all out of the west,
under the silver moon, sleep,
my little one, sleep, my pretty one, sleep."

Fighting on land, sea and in the air intensified. From all directions Allied forces closed in on Germany.

Russell, now Captain Marsh, and his crew returned from another gruelling mission on the first of May when word came that German radio was announcing Hitler had died defending Berlin against the Russians.

"Listen up, guys, did I just hear what I thought I heard?" Richard was dumbfounded.

"If you heard that Hitler died defending Berlin, yes we heard that, too. But if you believe it you're more gullible than you look," Russell laughed.

"Do you think any of it is true?"

"Oh, he might be dead all right. But I don't believe for a minute he died in battle."

Russell's belief was proved valid a week later when Germany surrendered to the Allies and the truth of Hitler's suicide was made known.

* * *

Bumper to bumper motorists drove through the streets of town, horns blaring and people cheering. "V.E. Day! We won! Germany is beaten! The Third Reich is crushed!"

"Is the war over, dad?"

"It's over in Europe, John."

"Will Russ come home now?"

Jess smiled tiredly, "Soon, soon. It takes time to finish mopping up."

Eddie asked, "What about R.J.?"

"Unfortunately we're still fighting the Japs. The news from there isn't as hopeful. We're not through in the Pacific yet."

Jess and Naomi looked at each other. They had spent the better part of the last four years worrying constantly about their sons. And that worrying had taken its toll. The creases in their faces were deeper and it was getting harder to pretend that everything would be all right.

Naomi sighed and took Jess's hand in hers. She didn't say a word. She didn't need to.

* * *

Russell bounded up the three flights and knocked on the door, firmly holding the bouquet of roses he intended to surprise Moira with. Sydney opened the door and stood aside as he hurried inside. "Hi, Syd. Will you tell Moira I'm here."

Sydney hesitated. "It's good to see you, Russ. Sit down. I've got something to show you first."

She hurried from the room, returning quickly with a sleepy baby in her arms. Turning the baby to face Russ she said, "Here, darling, meet your daddy."

Russell found himself looking at an exact miniature replica of Moira's face. Sydney smiled, "Isn't he the handsomest one-year-old you've ever seen!"

Russell laid the flowers on the table and walked slowly toward them, pure joy shining in his eyes. He reached out to touch his son then tentatively pulled his hand back.

"Go ahead," Sydney laughed, "take him. He won't break."

As Russell grasped the baby gently she said, "I'll leave you two to get acquainted." She hurried from the room before Russ could see her tears.

The baby gave Russell a shy smile then his green eyes sparkled as he laughed aloud and said, "Da da."

Russell whirled him around the room. "My son! My son! You wonderful, beautiful boy!" He sat on the couch and bounced his son on his knee while the two of them chattered happily to each other.

On Sydney's return Russell said, "In every letter Moira has mentioned how much she appreciates you three for all you do for her and this little guy." He looked around, "Where is Moira anyway? Isn't she here?"

Quietly Sydney answered, "Russ, I have something to tell you and I don't quite know how to say it. But it's time you know."

Russell looked at her stricken face as a terrible dread filled his heart. "What? What is it?"

"Right up to the end," Sydney said sadly, "the buzz bombs kept coming. Moira had taken one load of injured children to hospital and was speeding through the streets for another run when a bloody bomb dropped . . ." Her voice trailed off as she watched the shock in his eyes.

"No," he whispered, "not Moira."

"She died instantly, Russ. She didn't suffer. She didn't suffer," Sydney repeated trying to ease his pain.

But he would not be comforted. Holding tightly to little Robert Jay, Russell sobbed in heart-wrenching agony.

> July 2, 1945
> Dear Uncle Duane,
> In some of your letters you mentioned how much Aunt Lucinda wants another baby. This terrible war has orphaned many children over here. If you're interested in adopting one, fill out the enclosed forms and send them to the London address listed on the front page. I talked to an international Red Cross worker here and she said, after I gave her your qualifications, she thought they could arrange for a baby for you. You'll need to act quickly if you're interested.
> If you do get a baby from here it will be delivered to you by an agency worker. Apparently they've done quite a bit of this. I think you'll have to meet her at the airport in Salt Lake to pick up the baby. They usually go to the major airports only.
> I'm leaving here soon and will send my new address as soon as I know it. Thanks for all you've done for mom and dad. They appreciate you two and so do I.
> Love, Russ

> July 7, 1945
> Dear Mom and Dad,
> My unit is being shipped to the Pacific. We leave in

the morning. We're supposed to stop in Hawaii for a few days before being reassigned further. I'll send my change of address as soon as I can.

Don't worry about me. Everything is fine. It's good to have the fighting over with here. The people here (I'm in London now) are starting to realize they don't have to fear the sound of airplanes anymore. Although some of them will never get over the horrors they've suffered.

I have no idea where I'll be but if I do run into R.J. we'll have a reunion to write home about. Tell Eddie and John and Belle to listen carefully to the news so they can understand what freedom and peace mean without having to learn it the hard way. I hope I never have to go through another war.

Give everyone my love. I'll see you one of these days.

Love, Russ

* * *

"So you're riding shotgun this time, huh?"

"Yes," answered Russell, "just like my great great grandpa did a hundred years ago. But the coach is a tad different."

Richard laughed, "You can say that again. Which plane are you chaperoning?"

Russell pointed, "That one over there."

"What's her payload?"

"One bomb."

"Just one?! What good will one bomb do?"

Russell smiled, "I haven't the foggiest. They just call it 'Little Boy' and claim it'll change the course of the war."

"That's incredible! One bomb to put the ball in our court? I find that hard to believe."

"I do too, but mine is not to reason why and all that." He turned to leave then stopped and looked seriously at his friend. "You won't forget about the packet, will you?"

Richard grinned. "Not with all the reminders you've given me. But not to worry. You'll come back and deliver it yourself."

Russell's P-51 Mustang flew smooth and sweet as he kept the larger plane in view. He looked again at the map. Yep, they were nearly on target. Hiroshima. *Wonder who picked that town out of the hat.* Subconsciously he watched as the Enola Gay's bomb bay doors opened.

Russell's earphones crackled, "Turn back now, Green Eyes."

The disembodied voice called again, more urgently this time, "Turn back! Turn back! Let's get out of here! Pronto!"

But Russell didn't hear the warning. His gaze was locked onto a vision beyond the falling bomb.

The Mustang jolted violently then fell, spinning, into the mushroom shaped cloud rising from the earth below.

* * *

"Mr. Marsh? Mr. Duane Marsh?"

"Yes." Puzzled Duane looked at the tall young airman.

"My name is Richard Bartolino. I have something for you, sir." He hesitated. "It's something Russ asked me to give you when I got back to the states."

"Come in. sit down, " Duane nodded toward a nearby chair. "Can I get you something? Root beer? Orange juice?"

The solemn faced Captain shook his head. "No thanks. I can't stay long. I've got to get back to Salt Lake. My plane leaves tonight."

He pulled a thick packet from his briefcase and handed it to Duane. "Russ and I were in the same outfit," tears glistened in his eyes. "He was the finest man I've ever known.

"I promised him I'd hand these things to you directly. He told me to ask you to go through them when you're alone. Then you can decide what to do from there."

Duane took the packet and gently traced his finger across Russell's familiar handwriting. Memories of Russ growing up with his smile and trusting ways filled Duane's mind. They had been so very close.

"Well sir," Richard gripped Duane's hand firmly, "I'll be on my way. I'm sure you'll find comfort in his papers." He turned and walked out of the house closing the door quietly behind him.

After a long time, Duane stood and walked thoughtfully up the rise behind the house to the tree where he and Russ had talked so often. Resting his back against the trunk, he slowly broke the seal on the packet. Placing the contents carefully on his lap Duane unfolded the top page and began to read.

Dear Uncle Duane,

I've asked my friend to deliver these things if I don't come back. I'd tell you myself if I could but this is the only other alternative I can think of. I've always loved and admired you. That's why I'm writing this to you.

I wonder if you've already guessed that the baby you adopted is my son. I loved his mother with all my heart and hoped to take her home with me after the war and work something out so we could be married. She was the most decent, caring, unpretentious human being I have ever known. She was killed in a bomb blast just before the war ended. You'll find her genealogy, family pictures and a brief history of her I've written in this packet. If you decide at some time to tell my son about me I ask you to please let him read about his mother, too. He was named after her brother who died in the war.

I kept in touch with the woman who brought him to you so I know you call him by his middle name. And, knowing you, I'm sure you've taken him into your heart as you did me. I can't tell you how much that means to me. I know mother and dad don't have the health to take him and I want to make sure Cora never gets her hands on him. I hope she never learns of him. That's why I couldn't say anything before.

Read the documents and letters and look at the pictures. If you decide to tell him about his mother and father someday, I hope and pray he'll understand and know how very much we love him and each other.

Thanks again for all you've done and are. Till we meet again.

Love, Russ

Chapter Seven

Forget Me Not

Saturday, August 10th, 11:40 a.m.

"Tell me something, Mandy, did the twins ever trick you before you got married?"

Ray interrupted, laughing, "Not a chance. We tried to a couple of times but it never worked."

Amanda glanced at Ray, grinning, "They fooled just about everybody." She smiled at Jay, "But I was so nuts about this silly guy I knew every detail about him. He's right, they never did trick me."

Jay gave her a hug and shook Ray's hand. "It's great to see you again. Take care."

He worked his way back to their table and sat down beside Duane and Melissa.

"Hi, brother," Melissa embraced him, "is my favorite niece coming?"

Jay saw his daughter's car pulling into the parking lot. "She sure is. There she is now."

Melissa hurried toward the little group getting out of the car. "I'm so glad you made it! Let me help with the children."

She stepped forward and took the baby as Moira reached back into the car to lift the two-year-old out of his car seat.

"Thanks Aunt Missy. Dave's on call this weekend so I've been wrestling these two by myself this time." She laughed, "Actually, they've been pretty good little travelers."

Jay and Duane reached the car and Moira watched fondly as Jay lifted Russell Jay into his arms.

"Hi gampa!" grinned Russ.

"Hi yourself, my little buddy. How are you?"

Moira reached up and kissed Jay. "He's fine and full of ginger," she laughed, "and so am I."

She turned and kissed Duane. "Hi granddad. It's sure good to see you again."

Duane smiled warmly at this bonus granddaughter. "It's good to see you, too, sweetheart."

Russ wriggled to get down to run to Darlene who was hurrying toward them.

Jay took nine-month-old Lucinda from Melissa. "Hi, my sweet Lucy. Give grandpa a kiss."

They all walked back to the table and sat down, Lucinda bouncing happily on Jay's knee.

"How was the drive from Ogden?"

"Great, mom. These two slept most of the way, thank heavens. And traffic wasn't bad so we made good time."

Duane got to his feet and started toward Ted who was headed in their direction, his limp scarcely noticeable.

"They never did fix his leg completely, did they?" Melissa asked quietly.

"No," Jay replied. "They did their best but the damage was too severe."

Ted greeted them warmly then turned, "This can't be little Moira, surely?"

"In the flesh," she laughed as she hugged him. "I wasn't sure you'd remember me."

"Your green eyes are too memorable to forget. Besides that, you really haven't changed much. But it is hard to believe you're old enough to have two children."

"Did your family come with you?" asked Duane.

"Yes. Dad drove them up above town to see if they could find the place he used to swim when he was a kid. They've all heard about that so much they wanted to see it. They should be back any minute."

Duane pointed, "Is that them coming up the road there?"

"Yes it is. I'd better go help them get the car unloaded."

"I'll come with you," Duane said. "I need to stretch my legs." He turned to the others, "I'll be right back."

They watched the two men stroll across the grass, their heads close together in companionship as they reminisced.

Chapter Eight

Ted

"Come in Uncle Duane. I'm glad you got here okay. Did your meetings go well?"

"They were fine but I can tell I'm slowing down. I'm not as fond of being away from home any more. Traveling gets a little harder each year." Duane grimaced, "I think it'll soon be time for me to retire and let the younger generation take over."

As they stepped into the sun warmed living room Duane could see more clearly the haggard look on Sam's face. "Still no word from Ted?"

Sam answered sadly, "He finally called last night. He's in Phoenix."

"Phoenix? What's he doing there?"

"He says he's thinking of going to school there."

There was so much left hanging in Sam's answer, Duane was sure there was more to it. But, before he could continue, they heard voices coming from the hall.

"That'll be mother and Helen," Sam said quietly. "Mother has been real anxious for you to get here." They turned as Ila Mae came into the room followed by Sam's wife.

Ila Mae walked quickly over and hugged Duane. "I'm so glad you're here, even though you must be anxious to get home."

"It's good to see you again." Duane included Helen in his smile.

As they settled into comfortable chairs Duane thought about Ila Mae. He was only eleven years old when she was born to Everett and Minnie and more than once he'd been her confidant during her rollicking teen years. Both she and her sister Bea had given their parents some worrisome times before they settled down with families of their own.

Now she was at the other end of the stick as they all worried about Sam's and Helen's oldest son.

Ted was born in 1950, the year after Sam and Helen moved from Creekston to Middle Fork. He was an honor student all through his school years, was a high school football star and an Eagle Scout. He'd always been popular with his peers yet had never lost sight of his family loyalties.

Lucyann and Trish, his younger sisters, had adored him from the time they were infants. Friends and family began calling them The Three Musketeers before Trish could walk.

Ted joined the army right out of high school two years ago. He told his family that the war wouldn't last long and he'd just as soon get his service time behind him so he could get back and get on with his life. Much as they hated to have him go, they agreed with his decision and reasoning.

After basic training he was shipped directly to Vietnam. At first his letters seemed upbeat, typically Ted. He didn't tell them much about the war, just talked about the friends he was making and a little about some of the Vietnamese children he'd befriended. Then his letters became shorter and more vague, leaving many unanswered questions.

Sam and Helen and Ila Mae, who had moved in with them after Theo died, listened to every newscast and read every newspaper article about the situation in Vietnam. Sam's heart murmur had kept him out of the service during the Korean conflict so he didn't have a frame of reference concerning personal military life.

But his memories of growing up were vivid with stories of his Uncle Ed and cousins R.J. and Russ who were fighting in World War II. The stories he remembered about them and that war didn't resemble this war in Vietnam much. He had thought Ted was doing the right thing, the patriotic thing, when he joined the army. But he wasn't so sure any more. It got more confusing every time they listened to the news.

Then they got word Ted had been injured and was being sent to a hospital in the states. When he was finally transferred to the Veterans Hospital in Salt Lake they were able to visit with him.

"He was so changed," Sam said sadly. "It wasn't his injuries. They were healing."

"No," Helen added, "except for a limp, his physical health was good." She brushed away a tear. "He was just so different. Not the same smiling, carefree Ted who had left home the year before."

"Even when we took Lucyann and Trish to see him, hoping they would be able to cheer him up, the smiles he gave them never reached his eyes," Sam continued. "The doctors talked about post traumatic stress and words like that, and told us to give him time. But the little while he was home didn't help."

"He pretended everything was fine," Helen said, "but we couldn't seem to reach him any more. He seemed locked in a dark place and we couldn't help him get out. At night we heard him pacing but when we got up and tried to talk to him he told us he was okay, just a little restless."

Sam said slowly, "Then one morning he was gone. He'd put some of his clothes in his army duffle bag, left a note on his bed saying not to worry that he'd get in touch with us, and slipped out of the house without a sound. That's when we called and asked if you and the rest of the family would pray for him."

Duane shook his head thoughtfully. "I don't know how you've stood it these past four months. It broke our hearts when our little Russ died nearly thirty years ago. But at least we were with him and knew what was happening. To not know where your child is has to be terrible. How did Ted sound when he called last night?"

"About the same as he was before he left. He apologized and tried to sound upbeat but we could still hear the emptiness in his voice." Sam paused, "But at least we know he's okay and where he is."

Ila Mae said quietly, "I wonder why Phoenix? I wonder what made him choose Phoenix?"

* * *

Ted watched the protesters straggle into the area across from the administration building. Some were carrying signs, others were trying to get the large poster of President Nixon into position so they could burn it.

He smiled grimly. He'd seen it all before. He should be used to it by now.

But each time, as the flames consumed the picture or the flag or the effigy of Uncle Sam, all he could see were the faces of his buddies who hadn't come back. The faces of those he hadn't been able to save.

He intended to walk away. Instead he leaned against the trunk of the tree he was under and slowly sat down on the grass putting his face in his hands, willing his mind to go blank and his heart to slow down until he could gain control of himself.

"You okay?"

The voice seemed to come from deep within his soul.

Another bad dream, Ted thought, as he shook his head to clear it.

But when he opened his eyes he saw an apparition in bright gossamer shimmering in the dappled light of the tree under which he was huddled. Giving a low moan, Ted once again dropped his head into his hands as the figure floated toward him.

"You really had me worried," Penny said. "Your face went so pale I thought you were going to pass out."

"Well, you kinda surprised me," Ted answered warily, "I thought I was having a nightmare."

He looked around frowning, "What happened to all the others?"

Penny laughed, "Oh, we never stick around once we've made our point."

"WE? You're one of those peaceniks?"

"Yes," she nodded, "we believe in peace, not war." Then she added, puzzled, "I thought you saw me arrive with the others. You were staring at us with such ferocity."

He wasn't about to tell her about his blackouts. He considered them a sign of weakness, one he preferred to keep to himself.

"How long has everybody been gone? And why are you still here?"

"Not long. And I'm not sure why I'm here. I saw you still sitting here when we finished. You didn't move, didn't even seem to be breathing. Then, when we were leaving I turned and saw you still slumped here." She dropped her eyes. "I don't know why I came over. I thought you might need help or something. Then when you looked up at me I thought you were having a heart attack."

"No such luck," Ted said bitterly. "With the sun behind

you and the breeze blowing your white dress...you just didn't look real. I thought I was dreaming."

"Yeah, I know. You said nightmare." She hesitated, "Is that what we are to you, a nightmare?"

He looked hard at her. "You better believe it! That's exactly what all of you are to me."

* * *

"Io sono, tu sei, lui/lei é, noi siamo, voi siete, loro sono. Damn," Ted muttered as he walked across the campus toward his apartment after his evening class, "I'll never get these verbs memorized." *Quit complaining,* he told himself, *you wanted something to take your mind off the nightmares. Just concentrate and don't blow it now.*

He continued along the dimly lit walk forcing his mind to continue conjugating Italian verbs. "Io servo, noi serviamo, io capisco, noi capiamo." *Yeah, right! I served, but I sure as hell don't understand any longer!*

"Stop it, you jerk! I said stop!"

Ted halted instantly. Then he realized the words weren't directed at him. They were coming from deep within the dark alley between the two buildings.

"Let me go!" An edge of panic tinged the fury.

"Come on, babe, you know you want it as much as I do. I've waited a long time for this."

The sounds of scuffling escalated reminding Ted of night sounds in the jungle. *None of my business,* he thought. *If these dumb broads want to play hard to get they shouldn't be surprised when some stud calls their bluff.*

As he turned away from the alley, a muffled scream was cut off abruptly as the sound of a body hitting the ground came clearly through the darkness. "Gotcha!" snarled a triumphant bellow.

Ted pivoted into the blackness of the alley without another thought, rushing toward the shadowy figures ahead. He could see a girl prone on the ground with a man kneeling over her, unbuckling his belt.

Ted slammed into him with all the force and skills he had learned in combat, knocking the surprised attacker against the wall before he realized what was happening.

All the rage Ted had kept bottled up for months came barreling to the surface. His fists pummeled and pounded the struggling form trying to crawl away.

"Stop!" From far away words swam through the red miasma fogging his mind. "Stop! You're killing him!"

The hand on Ted's arm shook him convulsively trying to get his attention. Ted hesitated, watching through half shuttered eyes as the battered figure braced against the wall slowly slid to the ground.

Ted shook his head doggedly trying to clear his mind and gain control of himself.

"Come on, hurry before the campus cops find us." She tugged at Ted's arm trying to drag him back out onto the walk.

He stumbled after her. Glancing back he asked, "What about him?"

"Don't worry about him. He's alive. He's just going to be real sore for a few days."

They made their way quickly to the corner and turned down a small street leading away from campus.

"Come on," she continued to tug at his sleeve. "I need something to settle my nerves. Let's go there." She pointed toward a small Trattoria on the next corner.

"We must both look a mess," she continued, "but I know the owners and they won't ask dumb questions."

They were seated at a small candle lit table in the back

corner of the room before Ted got himself completely under control and looked at the girl across from him.

"You!" he said with such animosity Penny cringed. "What the hell do you think you're doing!"

Her eyes blazed. "What do I think I'm doing? You're just as bad as that jerk back there! I was trying to save you from having to explain to the cops why you nearly killed Jack."

"Jack! You mean you know that jerk? You didn't need help?"

She lowered her head and answered quietly, "Yes, I guess I did need help. I thought I could handle him. I was wrong. I'm sorry I got you into this. You can leave now. I'll be okay."

Ted stood up, nearly knocking over his chair. Then, noticing her sagging shoulders, he sat back down. "Sorry. I shouldn't have reacted like that. I do appreciate not getting involved with the police. But I'm still confused. You want to tell me about this?"

"There's not much to tell," Penny said sadly. "Jack has been after me for a long time to go out with him. I've tried to put him off every way I know how. Finally I agreed to a date tonight." She paused. "He said first he wanted to show me something in the library so, like a dope, I took the shortcut through that alley with him. I realized too late that all he wanted to show me was what a great lover he is. I told him to knock it off but my resistance just seemed to excite him.

"When he threw me on the ground it knocked the wind out of me. The next thing I knew a banshee was screaming down the alley and I heard blows I thought would never stop. Where did you learn to fight like that, anyway?"

"You don't want to know. Trust me on that." Ted hesitated. "Will he give you any more trouble?"

"I don't think so. I think you scared him worse than you did me."

"Well, you'd better watch your back from now on just to make sure."

Suddenly his face softened and he asked quietly, "Since we're here do you want to eat something?"

Penny answered slowly, "I wouldn't say no. Actually, I'm starved. I thought Jack was taking me out to eat so I didn't bother with lunch." She grinned ruefully, "I won't make that mistake again."

While they ate, feeling uncharacteristically shy, Penny darted quick glances at Ted. She liked what she saw. His deep brown eyes were in striking contrast with the golden highlights flickering in the candlelight through his blond hair. His jaw was strong, yet vulnerable, and his nose was just crooked enough to add to his rugged good looks. He was taller than she was by a good six inches and his broad shoulders couldn't quite be hidden under his loose denim jacket.

If he didn't have such a fierce intensity, she thought, *he'd be very attractive.* Then she realized he was watching her.

"Am I that scary?" he asked quietly.

Penny prided herself on being straightforward so she wouldn't equivocate now. "Not scary," she answered slowly, "intimidating."

Good, he thought. *Better intimidating than weak.* "If you're through, come on and I'll walk you home."

"You don't need to do that."

"Yeah, I do. I don't want to have to rescue you again tonight from a frustrated Jack."

They sat on the front steps of her apartment building, relaxed in the warm night air. Ted's thoughts were in tight control now. No way was he going to get involved with anyone at this point in time. Especially a flower child.

"A penny for your thoughts," she said quietly.

"Just thinking how quiet it is here. How peaceful."

"You were in Vietnam, weren't you?"

He tensed. "What makes you think so?" he asked tightly.

"I'm not sure. You're not like the other guys. You don't look very old, but sometimes you seem ancient."

"Well, since you asked, yes I was in Vietnam. And no, it's none of your business."

"I know," she said solemnly. "You've already said I was a nightmare. But why are you so angry? Couldn't you get a deferment?"

"I didn't even try. I come from a real patriotic, gung ho family." He added cynically, "We always serve our country. We've always agreed with whoever said 'my country, right or wrong.' Well, that's what I thought, too. Only I never figured on the 'wrong' part."

"Then I don't understand. Why do you hate those of us who protest the war so much?"

"Because you're self serving, selfish jerks. You haven't a clue what it's like over there. You sit here in your safe little world and denounce those grunts over there without a second thought.

"You parade around in your self righteousness, condemning those of us who were sent over there without so much as a by-your-leave. Marching around like you do not only hurts those who are over there, it helps the very enemy they're fighting. No thanks, I don't understand where you're coming from and I never will!"

He arose and strode rigidly up the road without a backward glance.

* * *

Dear Mom & Dad,

I'm fine. I'm only taking 3 classes so the work isn't too hard. I got a job in a little Italian cafe not far from campus. It will help me practice the language. I buss tables now but will work up to waiter if I stay there.

Don't worry about sending money. My GI benefits & the job cover what I need. Tell Trish & Lucyann 'hi.' I hope Lucyann likes BYU. Thanks for your letters. Yes, protesters show up on this campus sometimes, too. I just ignore them.

Love, Ted

* * *

"Ciao, Ted, come va?"

"Abbastanza bene, e tu?"

"Bene, grazie. Novita?"

"Niente di speciale, Pete, just trying to keep up. How did you ever learn all the conjugations and tenses?"

Pietro grinned, "Italian is all I ever heard until I was four years old. Then i miei genitori figured I wouldn't do very well in school if I couldn't speak inglese, so they hired a tutor and insisted we all speak English until we had it down pat. Between that and the words I'd already picked up from TV and the kids in the neighborhood, it didn't take long."

"Well, I wish it wouldn't take so long for me. I've been in that class over two months now and I still don't know merda."

Pietro roared with laughter. "Where'd you learn that? Not in your Italian class, I bet."

"One of my buddy's parents came from Palermo. He used to say that all the time. That was his favorite expression when something went wrong. We all picked it up from him."

Pietro noted the past tense but, hearing the sadness in

Ted's voice, didn't pursue it. "Dad said to thank you for coming in early. We've got to put those tables together over by the window and get set up for a bunch coming in."

Ted ignored the noisy chatter around the long table as he worked to keep other tables cleared and water glasses filled. He heard bits and pieces of conversations as he put dirty dishes in the container and washed off a nearby table. But one discussion made him stop and listen.

"Did you hear about your great admirer, Penny?"

"What are you talking about? What admirer?"

"The one who's been pestering you to go out with him."

There was a long pause. Then, softly, "Jack?"

"Of course Jack," Marti laughed, "who else? Tom said he showed up wild eyed one night a while back looking like he'd been dragged through a patch of mesquite bushes. He claimed he was going home where he could earn some money, he was sick and tired of school. No one's seen him since. They're guessing he crossed somebody he couldn't bully and turned tail and ran."

Ted turned slowly and met Penny's eyes. He gave a quick wink and carried the loaded receptacle into the kitchen.

Later, Ted worked to clear and dismantle the long table while the patrons lined up to pay the cashier. He mentally rehearsed the list of verbs he needed to memorize. Although he ignored the group, he clearly overheard their comments.

"Who's that hunk?"

"You mean the guy cleaning up?"

"Yeah, him. He's gorgeous."

"Right on, but I don't think he's your type, Marti."

"Maybe not, but I'd sure be willing to give him a try."

Penny remained silent during this discussion, resisting the temptation to look back and see if Ted heard her friends.

She hoped not. It seemed demeaning to discuss him like that while he was within earshot.

As she lay in bed later she wondered what had happened to Ted to make him so cynical and antisocial. She had run into him a few times since the night he came to her rescue, but he always just nodded slightly and walked on. He seemed lonely and sad as though he was carrying some overwhelming burden. She had met a few other veterans since coming here to school, but none of them were as solitary and strange as Ted.

Ted tossed and turned, trying for sleep. The image of auburn hair curling softly around a saucy face with clear blue eyes, a playful smile and a nose sprinkled lightly with freckles swam into his mind every time he closed his eyes. No way, he reminded himself. No way do I want to get involved with an empty headed peacenik who stands for everything I hate.

He thought of his friends in 'Nam who hadn't made it back. There was no earthly reason why he should still be alive when those guys were dead. *And there's no way Penny and her friends could ever understand what it's like over there. She's not worth a second thought.*

But second thoughts and third thoughts and fourth thoughts swirled inside his head as he burrowed deeper in bed trying to get to sleep.

Two days later Penny caught up with Ted as he left work. "Mind if I walk a ways with you?"

"It's a free country."

She stepped in front of him, forcing him to stop. "Why do you do that?"

"Do what?"

"Don't be obtuse. You know what I mean." Penny sighed, "I don't want to quarrel with you. Why can't you accept a simple friendly gesture?"

Ted stepped around her and continued walking, his eyes straight ahead. He muttered, "I'm here to go to school, not to make friends."

"Well why in the world can't you do both?" She lengthened her stride to keep up with him.

He turned onto his block and paused. He knew he was acting like a total jerk.

"I apologize." He nodded toward his apartment, "Do you want to come in? It's not much but it beats living in a dorm."

Inside he waited until she sat down then asked, "Is Pepsi okay? It's all I've got."

"Sure," she laughed, "as long as it's not poisoned."

"There's not much to tell," he said in answer to her query. "I grew up in a little town in Utah, joined the army right out of high school, and was in 'Nam a little over a year."

"Does your leg bother you much?"

"Only when I'm running after bad guys and bussing tables." He shrugged, "Sorry. Bad joke. I don't think about it most of the time. But tell me about you. Are you from here?"

"No." She laughed, "You're not going to believe this, but I'm from Utah, too."

"You're pulling my leg."

"I really am. We lived in Ogden until I was in sixth grade. Then we moved to Provo. My family still lives there."

"Well why are you going to school down here?"

"I just felt stifled and wanted to see how it was someplace else. I didn't have the courage to go too far away so Phoenix seemed about right."

"I don't want to start an argument but how do your folks feel about your political views?"

"That was one of the problems. My family is pretty conservative. They're waiting for me to come to my senses and come back to Zion."

"And what do you think about that?"

"I still feel like I'm right about the way the government is run. But I don't feel so rebellious about everything else any more. Who knows, maybe I'll go back after graduation. I haven't decided yet." She looked at Ted, "What about you? Will you go home again?"

"I don't know," he answered quietly. "Not until I have more answers than questions."

Banners were posted all over town. *A person couldn't avoid them even if he wanted to,* Ted thought.

ANTI-WAR RALLY THURSDAY!
Meet in front of ROTC Bldg 2 p.m.
Nixon sends troops into Cambodia to
'save lives & shorten the conflict.'
JOIN WITH US TO PROTEST THESE LIES!

"You planning to join the protest?"

Ted scowled, "Not a chance! What about you, Pete?"

"Naw. I'll have too much to do here." He grinned, "Protesters are always hungry after a big rally."

Ted walked slowly around the wave of humanity moving across the quad. He had left class early in order to avoid the crowds but the protesters started arriving earlier than expected, making his progress off campus virtually impossible.

As he worked his way through the milling, jostling mass

Ted recognized an ugly undercurrent and wondered what it would take to turn the crowd into an uncontrollable mob.

He knew professional organizers had been brought in from California. The difference between this teeming horde and the local protests he had observed was like the difference between night and day. There was a fervency here he didn't trust.

He finally made it to the outer fringe where the crowd was thinning out. But even here the atmosphere was grim. As he edged around the last of the stragglers, he found himself face to face with Penny.

"You better watch yourself today. That's a tough bunch your group has invited here."

Her eyes flashed with irritation. "Tough times call for tough measures. Nixon had no business escalating things over there."

"I can't argue with that. I just think you guys might have bit off more than you can chew this time."

"Well, what would you have us do—pat Tricky Dicky on the head and say 'naughty, naughty?' You think I don't understand the situation over there. And you're probably right. But it seems to me there are a whole lot of our guys dying over there for nothing.

"Tell me something honestly. Do you really support this hypocrisy of calling it a 'police action?'" Disgust filled her voice, "The government doesn't even have the guts to call it what it is—WAR!"

Ted's mind flashed back to a similar discussion as he, Clyde, Tomas, Scuz and Benjie worked their way carefully forward. They were the point men, sent ahead of the rest of the squad as scouts. Scuz had just asked the difference between a 'police action' and a regular war when they emerged from the trees into a small clearing with a handful of primitive houses grouped together. Three grinning Vietnamese adolescents stood facing them in front of the first house.

Before Ted could call out a warning Tomas, fresh from the states, stepped forward and said, "Hey, amigos," his hand outstretched in greeting. Instantly all hell broke loose. The youths dropped to the ground firing guns they had hidden behind their backs while gunfire erupted from every window and door of the village.

It wasn't long before the full squad arrived and secured the area but it seemed like an eternity. And when the helicopter lifted off later it carried Scuz, Tomas and Clyde in body bags.

Scuz never did get his question answered, thought Ted bitterly.

"Hey! Earth to Ted! You still here?"

Ted's vision cleared. "Yeah, I'm still here. But not for long. See you around." He jogged away trying to put as much distance between him and the crowd as possible.

A burst of static preceded a fierce, agitated torrent of words amplified to megawatt decibels. One of the invited agitators, Ted surmised, psyching up the crowd to the desired pitch. Same song, second verse— "down with Nixon, down with General Abrams, down with the war, and especially down with U.S. baby killing soldiers!"

Ted was sick of hearing that kind of garbage. He couldn't get away from there fast enough. But even in his rush he couldn't help but notice the just arrived young Coast Guard troops standing stiffly, nervously fingering their weapons. *A recipe for trouble,* Ted thought, *I hope Penny realizes the seriousness of her situation.*

His next thought was anger at himself. Why should I care

what she's got herself into? If she's going to play with matches she'd better be prepared to get her fingers burned.

Ted was only a couple of blocks from campus when the sound of explosions came in rapid succession. They were followed by a moment of eerie silence, then a burst of sporadic gunfire coupled with screams and mass confusion.

"What the hell?" Ted muttered as he turned. He saw a sea of humanity rushing away from campus in every direction. He reached out and grabbed the arm of a running student, yelling, "What happened?"

Fear and confusion were written all over the young man's face. "Somebody exploded something! Then shooting started!" He tore his arm from Ted's grasp, "I gotta get away from here!"

The image of Penny's trusting yet determined face flashed into Ted's mind. He ran back toward campus, shoving people out of his way in his haste. When he got near the spot he had last seen Penny, he saw two screaming, crying coeds kneeling over a form on the ground. Ted ran closer and saw Penny lying still, her eyes closed, blood staining her white sweatshirt.

He dropped to her side and expertly felt for a pulse. It was very faint. He knew she needed help immediately.

"Go for help!" he barked, but the two students continued rocking back and forth, moaning in shock.

Ted sprang to his feet and ran toward a uniformed figure. "Get an ambulance! Hurry!" he ordered then, as the guardsman ran toward the closest building, turned and rushed back to where Penny lay.

"Dear God," he whispered, holding her hand tightly, "if you're there, don't let her die. Not like this."

But even as he said the words he thought of all the other times in the midst of battle he had prayed these words and was afraid the answer would be the same this time.

Ted leaned against the wall in the emergency waiting room. He knew from experience Penny's chances were slim. *That damned war,* he thought, *it kills them over there and it kills them over here. Will it never stop?*

Hours later he watched as a doctor, old and tired, walked toward him. Ted hurried to meet him. "Is she going to make it?" he blurted out before the doctor could speak.

The doctor shook his head, "I don't know. We're doing all we can." He looked hard at Ted. "Are you the one who came in with her?" he asked kindly.

Ted nodded.

"Has someone contacted her family?"

Ted nodded again. "I gave the admitting nurse her parents' names. She said they would call them. Is there any way I can see her?"

The look on Ted's face told the doctor how important this was to him. "Come with me. I'll break the rules this once and let you see her for just a moment."

As Ted inspected Penny's ashen face, her body seeming much too small for the bed, his resolve to stay uninvolved fell away. It's too late NOT to care, he thought, and wished there was some way he could reach into that dark abyss which held her so he could tell her.

"I'm sorry," he whispered fervently, "so very sorry."

* * *

"It really is good to see you, Uncle Duane," Ted smiled crookedly, "even though I'm afraid it didn't sound like it when you called."

Duane laughed. "Well, my coming was a surprise to both of us. I'm not quite sure why headquarters thought I was the only one who could solve the problem." His expression turned serious, "But I have to admit I'm glad they called me here to Phoenix. It gave me a good excuse to see you again."

He hesitated, then decided to jump right in. "I've known you all your life, Ted, and I've never seen you so discouraged. Do you want to talk about it?"

"I'm not sure," Ted answered quietly. "Things don't make much sense these days."

Duane knew not to press. As much as he wanted to help, he knew the decision was Ted's to make. He watched with compassion as a single tear worked its way down Ted's cheek.

As he quickly brushed it away, Ted realized this was his opportunity to unburden himself, to find his way out of this maze in which he was trapped. Sitting here next to him was the one person in the world he trusted completely.

His words stumbled slowly at first then became a rushing torrent. He told Duane how terrible the disappointment was in Vietnam when they realized what a mess the government had gotten them into—that same government Ted had believed in so fiercely earlier.

He told how he had felt when he learned that one of their officers had been fragged by one of his own men, and of the babies that had been booby trapped by the Viet Cong so that when American soldiers picked up the crying infants they were blown to bits.

He told of trying to save injured buddies only to watch them die as they waited for rescue helicopters to arrive. And how his leg had been injured by bomb shrapnel from one of their own planes which had bombed the wrong coordinates. "Friendly fire. What an oxymoron!" he said disgustediy.

"And then in the hospital some of the guys told how they'd been cursed and spit on by our own citizens." Ted paused, "Maybe I could have accepted even that if I hadn't felt we were betrayed by our own government. It was like we were disposable, to be used and thrown away."

Ted told of the protests and demonstrations even here in this little corner of the world. As he talked about Penny's injuries, and that she was still in critical condition, his voice broke.

"That God I once believed in either doesn't care or isn't there," he said bitterly.

"Why do you say that?" Duane asked quietly.

"Because if there really is a God why does he hurt people so much?"

Duane asked softly, "Why are you blaming God for things men do?"

"Because he could stop them!" Ted answered vehemently.

"Yes, he could," Duane responded. "But if he did he wouldn't be God. He can't give man agency and then turn right around and take it away every time man does something stupid. You see, Ted, it isn't God that's the problem. It's man."

"I don't know, Uncle Duane. Just when things are beginning to make sense again, some jerk throws a string of lighted firecrackers into the middle of a crowd and the next minute innocent people get hurt just because they're there."

He looked steadily into Duane's eyes. "You've lived through hard times, lost children, parents, brothers . . . how have you reconciled all that with your belief in God?"

"I don't pretend it was easy. Like you, I've had plenty of questions. And I've been disillusioned and disappointed, too. Although I have to admit they didn't happen to me when I was as young as you are.

"But, as the years have gone by, I've come to realize that

I have to be responsible for myself. We all do. At some point in time we have to give up looking for reasons why things happen. We have to stop trying to place blame and get on with our lives."

Ted nodded slowly. "I want to believe that. I'm just not sure I can."

"It will come when you're ready, Ted. When you can put the past behind you. God put us here to learn and grow," Duane grinned, "and to take our lumps. He said, 'My peace I give unto you,' then went on to explain, 'not as the world giveth.' He knows the world's peace is transitory and that we'll find it tough sledding sometimes. But his peace is there. We just have to work for it and ask for it."

Chapter Nine

Peace

Saturday, August 10th, 11:50 a.m.

"You have found peace, haven't you?"

"Yes," Ted laughed, "It was there for the taking all the time. I finally recognized it when I looked deep inside myself and realized I didn't like what I saw." He stopped. "I couldn't have found it without you, you know."

Duane touched Ted's arm affectionately, "You'd have found it eventually anyway. I'm just glad you freed yourself from that load you were carrying."

They watched as the car pulled to a stop and doors flew open and Ted's family tumbled out.

"You should have gone with us, dad! It was real neat!"

Ted smiled. "I know. I remember swimming there, too, you know. Now come and help grandpa and me carry our things over to the table."

"Everything's in the trunk. I'm going to go ahead with Uncle Duane." Smiling broadly she put her arm through his. "We've got lots to catch up on."

"It's good to see you again, Penny. Did they ever find out if that bout of pneumonia last winter was related to your old bullet wounds?"

"Actually, they thought so but there's no way to know for sure. The fact that I seem prone to respiratory problems leads me to think there is some connection. But there's no sure proof."

"How do you deal with that?"

"I just try to take good care of myself. Last year I got too involved in too many projects." Penny laughed, "I'll try not to make that mistake again."

"Good." Duane patted her shoulder, "How are your parents? Do you see them very often?"

"Yes. Since they moved to St. George it's made the travel time much shorter. And since we've all learned to give a little things are much better. We see them quite often."

She put her arm around Duane's waist and smiled up at him, "Thanks again for helping Ted and me both get our priorities straightened out. You mean a lot to us."

"You both mean a lot to me, too." He hugged her gently.

Duane just got back to the table and was sitting down when all conversation stopped simultaneously throughout the pavilion as a sleek new Porsche pulled into a parking space and the doors slowly opened. Every eye was on the beautiful woman and slender adolescent who emerged.

Duane rose instantly and walked quickly toward the newcomers, his arms outstretched in welcome.

"Rose! I'm so glad you could make it!" His voice carried across the silence as a warning for everyone to get back to their business.

"And don't tell me this is Rafe?" he said, quieter now. "My goodness but you've grown. I hardly recognize you."

Raphael smiled shyly and returned Duane's hug. "Hi," he whispered, glad to see this man who always made him feel secure.

"It's good to see you, Uncle Duane," Rose said sincerely. "If you weren't here I'd be tempted to turn around and go back home."

"You mustn't feel that way. Your being here matters to all of us." He glanced at the relatives now back to laughing and talking with each other. "You'll just have to be patient and give everybody time. Things have a way of working out. Come on, you two, come and sit with us."

They started toward the pavilion as Melissa, Jay, Darlene and Moira reached them, quickly enveloping Rose and Raphael in their arms.

"Tim and Eddie," Melissa called, "come over here please."

The two boys called, "Hi, Rafe," as they took turns slapping palms and grinning. "Want to come and play frisbee?"

Raphael nodded and ran off with his cousins.

"Thanks, Missy," Rose said, "Rafe was worried about what people would think if we came today."

Melissa hugged her again, "I'm so glad you came. I can only guess how hard it's been for both of you. But you were right to come."

Rose sighed, "I know. That's why I was so determined. I know we're neither one going to find peace of mind until we can put this past year behind us." She smiled sadly, "But if your dad hadn't been here, I'm not sure I could have faced this."

Melissa patted her hand. "Dad's pretty special all right. He's been watching for you, afraid it might be too hard. But coming today was the best thing you could have done. This breaks the ice. And maybe from now on you can both get on with your lives."

Chapter Ten

Rose

"You've got a fine looking boy, Rose. How old is he?"

"Thanks Jay. Rafe just turned two."

Bradford bristled, "His name is Raphael, Rose. I told you I don't like nicknames."

Duane looked at Bradford thoughtfully. "I thought he was named after his grandpa."

"He is," Rose explained quickly. "Bradford doesn't like the name Rafe but agreed to Raphael, which is as close as I could come to grandpa's name."

Staring at her sternly Bradford said, "You don't have to discuss our personal business with people."

Rose looked startled, "People? These aren't just people! This is granddaddy's brother, Duane, and his son, Jay." Her eyes flashed with annoyance, "You've met them before."

Hoping to change the subject, Duane interjected, "It was good of you to come down for Lulabelle's funeral."

"I wouldn't miss it for the world, Uncle Duane. Aunt Lu was always so much fun. Whenever any of us kids needed a good laugh or a bit of nonsense, we could always get it from her." Rose turned to Jay, "Did Darlene come? I haven't seen her."

"She's in the other room helping with the flowers."

"Well, if you'll excuse me I think I'll run in and say hello. There's always so much activity after a funeral I might not get to see her then."

"We're not staying after, Rose. I told you that when we came," Bradford said angrily.

Rose tried to smooth things over. "I know. That's what I meant." Still holding Raphael, she hurried away.

Duane looked at Rose's husband. He was slightly built but carried himself in a way that made him look taller and more imposing. His brown eyes were hard and unsmiling as Rose walked away. He turned to follow her but Duane put his hand on his arm and asked, "Stewart? Is your family from around here? There were some Stewarts here when I was a kid."

"No!" Bradford answered firmly. "My family is from New England."

Duane was surprised. "I must be confused. I thought your family lived here in Utah."

Bradford frowned, "Well, my grandfather was born in Salt Lake, but his people came from Massachusetts."

Wondering why that was so important to him, Jay asked, "When did your ancestors come to Utah?"

"At the turn of the century. But in my home we were taught that, in reality, we're New Englanders and I've never questioned that."

"But don't you live in Salt Lake?"

"Yes, well, my work is there. But when the time is right I'll return to Massachusetts."

Hearing the resolve in his voice Duane queried, "And how does Rose feel about that?"

"I haven't the slightest idea. But her place is by my side so where I go, she goes."

What a strange, domineering young man, Duane thought. *How did Rose ever come to marry him?*

In the chapel Darlene hugged Rose and kissed little Rafe. "Oh, it's good to see you again. I know your mother is certainly glad you could come. She says she doesn't get to see you often enough since you got married and moved away."

Rose smiled. Convincing Bradford of the importance of coming today hadn't been easy but she was glad she had persisted. *Actually,* she mused guiltily, *it would have been nicer if he had stayed home and Rafe and I had driven down by ourselves.* But he had been adamant about coming so she hadn't pressed. It was enough that she was here.

As she listened to the words and music of the funeral, Rose's mind retraced the past four years. Marrying Bradford had seemed like a fairy tale come true. He was handsome and attentive and treated her like a queen.

No, she amended, not so much like a queen as like a valuable possession. At first she had been flattered by it, but she wasn't so sure any more. And after Rafe's birth Bradford had become more rigid, wanting to take complete control over their lives.

I do love him, she reminded herself. Maybe I'm the one who needs to lighten up a little. Maybe his concern is just his way of adjusting to the responsibility of having a family.

On the way back to Flagstaff two days later Darlene asked Duane, "Did you get a chance to visit with Ward's girl?"

"Very briefly. Bradford seemed to need to get home in a hurry so there wasn't much time. Rose sure looks good, doesn't she." It was stated in a way that needed no answer.

Jay spoke up, "She's turned into a real beauty. Her little boy certainly looks like her."

"Yes he does." Darlene added, "Aunt Maud seems kinda worried about her. Says she doesn't know about that man her granddaughter married."

"What did she mean?"

"She didn't say much. Just that he seems overly possessive."

So I'm not the only one who noticed, Duane thought. But he didn't voice his concern. His nephew, Ward, was always such a sweet kid. Duane had seen Ward's family as often as possible but with them living in Creekston and Duane's family in Flagstaff, opportunities to get together had been fewer than they had liked.

But Duane remembered little Rose well. She had always been such a good hearted little thing. *I wish I didn't have this nagging feeling about her husband,* he thought. *But I mustn't interfere. Rose has a good head on her shoulders. She'll work things out.*

* * *

Rose fought to stay awake. She sneaked a glance at her watch again. The speaker had been expounding for nearly two hours and still hadn't said anything worth hearing. She felt Bradford's disapproval as he moved slightly on the chair next to her. *All right, Rosie, sit up straight, take a deep breath and try to look interested!*

She trailed along behind Bradford as he worked his way through the crowd, stopping to talk to every person he considered important along the way. He didn't say two words to her as they made their way slowly toward the door. But she could feel his fury and knew what to expect when they got in the car.

"You could have at least pretended to be interested! Do you have any idea how many times you looked at your watch?"

Her anger flared, "And do you know how much sleep I got last night?" He didn't answer. "Do you?"

"I don't give a damn how much sleep you got! You could have tried to show some interest for my sake, if nothing else! How do you think I felt watching you nod off?"

"Bradford, let's not quarrel," she said tiredly. "I was up nearly all night with Raphael. His chicken pox nearly drove him up the wall. I'm tired. Let's just forget it."

He looked at her without a trace of compassion. "No. I won't forget it. That meeting was important to me. I want to get on the ticket. I told you how important Dr. Stevens is in the party. You are my wife. If you look bored when he's speaking, how the hell do you think that makes me look?"

"Well, maybe if either of you had ever sat up all night with a sick child, you would know what it feels like!"

They turned in the driveway. Bradford forced his features into the 'noble' expression she had seen so often lately and walked ahead of Rose into the house calling, "Mother, we're home."

His mother walked into the room stiffly erect, a position she often reminded her daughters to effect in order to look like the ladies she expected them to be. "Hello dear. How did the meeting go?"

He glanced frigidly at Rose, a look not lost on his mother. "As well as can be expected. How was Raphael?"

"Why, just fine. I don't know why you were worried, Rose, he hasn't made a sound all evening."

Exhausted, Rose smiled thinly. "That's good to hear Mother Stewart. Thank you for coming."

"It was no trouble at all." She nodded at Bradford, "I'll do anything I can to help my son's career along." She smiled with cold superiority, sensing the tension between the two before her, "After all, that's what we women were put on earth for—to stand behind our men and help them succeed."

Bradford smiled smugly, "Come on, mother, I'll drive you home."

Rose walked upstairs and into Raphael's bedroom. He lay in bed stiffly, his eyes wide open.

"Hi, sweetie. How'd it go?"

"I'm glad you're home, mommy." He asked quietly, "Is gramma gone?"

"Yes. Daddy's taking her home." She looked at his face more closely. His teeth were tightly clenched, only his eyes moved. "What is it, Rafe? What's the matter?"

He burst into tears. "I'm sorry mommy. I'm sorry."

"For what, darling?"

"I tried so hard not to scratch. Gramma said if I moved one more time she would call and tell you not to come home tonight."

Rose gathered him into her arms, her own tears perilously close. "Oh darling. She didn't mean it. She just didn't want you to scratch off the scabs and be scarred. She would never do a thing like that." She rocked him gently and added, "And I'll always come home. You can count on it."

She held him in her arms until he finally fell into a fitful sleep. *Never again,* she vowed, *never again will I go leave a sick child with that block of granite, regardless of how important it is to support my husband without fail.*

She was in bed pretending to be asleep when Bradford got home. She was too tired to confront him with his mother's threats, knowing it wouldn't do any good anyway. His family lived by an inflexible code of behavior. The men were the head of the house and the women supported them in everything. His mother and father set the example and his two sisters and their husbands followed suit. Again Rose wondered if she was the one out of step.

Next evening, after Raphael had fallen asleep, Rose turned to Bradford, who was busily writing, and said, "Can we talk for a few minutes, honey?"

Irritated, he looked up, "Can't you see I'm busy?"

"Yes, but you're always busy. And we need to talk."

He put his pen down with careful precision and faced her with a look of patient tolerance, as though he were facing a recalcitrant child. "All right. Say what's on your mind. But make it short. I'm only halfway through."

Rose hurried into her message before she lost her nerve, "Bradford, I think it's time to have another baby."

"Another baby?" He looked at her like she had asked for the moon. "What are you talking about?"

"I want another baby," she said quietly. "Raphael is four now and will be going to school next year. You told me last year it was too soon." She plodded on, ignoring the angry color rising in his face, "I want more children, Bradford. Before we were married we talked of having at least three children. It's time for us to have another baby."

He forced himself to speak calmly. "Rose," he said very quietly and very deliberately, "I don't recall making any such statement about three children. I wanted a son and I've got a son. I don't need another son and I have no use whatsoever for daughters. Growing up with two sisters has convinced me that Raphael doesn't need the kind of distractions in his life I had in mine."

She was dumbfounded but determined to keep her voice under control. "Bradford, you did agree that we could have at least three children. I've never heard you say such things about having daughters. I can't believe what I'm hearing."

"Well, believe it. It's exactly how I feel."

"And what about me?" she asked sadly. "What about how I feel?"

"I can't help you. Your feelings are your problem, not mine."

She would not cry! Staring at a point on the wall beyond his shoulder she said, "Please, Bradford, I ask you to reconsider. Perhaps my timing in asking is bad. But I want another child."

He turned back to his papers and began writing. "That's tough because I couldn't give you another child if I wanted to. And I don't."

"What do you mean?"

"After Raphael was born and I knew for sure he was sound of mind and body, I had a vasectomy."

She shook her head to clear what she couldn't believe she had heard. "A what?"

"Don't be purposely dense. You know what a vasectomy is."

"Of course I know. I just can't believe you had one."

"Well I did."

"Without consulting me?"

"Why would I consult you?" He seemed genuinely puzzled. "It was my decision to make. You had nothing to do with it."

"I'm your wife, Bradford. What kind of man are you?"

"I'm the same man you married six years ago. And you were quite happy to become my wife then even though I wondered about the difference in our ages. So just drop it. I don't want to discuss it any more."

Rose left the room and stumbled blindly up the stairs. Who was this man she called husband? What had happened to them? He wasn't like this when we got married, was he? Was he? Try though she might, sleep wouldn't come that night.

As days turned into weeks, Rose was determined not to let Bradford's betrayal change her outlook on life. Her disposition was sunny by nature and she preferred to think of her cup as half full rather than half empty. She was bitterly disappointed about not having any more children but she believed in the sanctity of marriage so convinced herself to enjoy and be grateful for the child she had. Raphael was growing up to be a bright, cheerful boy and she refused to jeopardize his happiness with her own disappointment.

Even though Bradford was unyielding in his attitude concerning the role of family members, he was pleased with his son. He honestly believed he was treating Rose with fairness and was always surprised when she challenged his opinions. He felt that, given time, she would come to realize his opinions were intellectually superior to hers.

He enjoyed the envy in other men's eyes when they looked at her and knew she had the potential to become a prized asset. The auburn highlights in her softly curling hair, her brilliant hazel eyes and her calm, steadfast demeanor filled him with pride. Perhaps she was sometimes headstrong but that could be attributed to her youth and lack of experience.

She was twenty-four to his thirty-five when they married. At that time he was already confidently established on the path he had set out for himself. He knew that marriage to the right woman would enhance his plans for success. When he met Rose he was physically attracted to her and was sure he could turn her youth to his benefit as he molded her to fit his plans.

Rose looked at the difference in their ages through the eyes of romance and was confidant they could adjust those differences to make a good marriage. She had always been mature for her age and more sagacious than her peers so she had no qualms about marrying an older man.

So, to all appearances, the family continued to function happily. And they were happy for the most part. With patience and wit on Rose's part, irritations were soon smoothed over. Bradford not only got on the ticket but when the election was held in November he won a seat in the state legislature by a large margin.

Rose purposefully kept busy. She was a gracious hostess for the many parties and functions Bradford felt were important to his career and her time with Raphael was a joy to them both. She took him to the park, the zoo, children's programs, church activities and spent every evening possible reading to him at bedtime.

As the time for Raphael to enroll in kindergarten approached, Rose remembered the Dean's words to her when she left the University of Utah Humanities Department at the time of her marriage. "If you ever decide to teach again let me know and if there's not an opening in the Art History section, I'll create one for you."

She had taken classes toward her PhD earlier. Maybe now was the time to get the work completed. She could teach a couple of classes, too, which would give her a measure of financial independence to pursue her goal.

"Bradford, I'm thinking of returning to my teaching job on a part time basis in the fall while Raphael is in school."

Bradford's hands paused over the papers he was sorting and he looked sternly at her. "No, Rose. No wife of mine is going to work."

She felt she was caught in a time warp. "I'll only be gone the hours Raphael is in school." She paused then added, "This is the nineties, you know. Many wives work these days."

"Not my wife! No! I forbid it!"

It was times like this that tried Rose's patience. "I'm not your possession, Bradford. And you're not my father giving me an ultimatum."

His face froze. "I'm not trying to be your father. I'm telling you that you will not work outside our home. And that's the end of it. I don't care to discuss this any further."

Rose looked up to see Raphael standing in the doorway. *All right, Bradford,* she thought, *I won't quarrel with you in front of Rafe, but you've not heard the end of this.* Brightly, she said, "Hi sweetie, come on in."

Warily he stepped into the room. His parents didn't air their differences in front of him but he was old enough to sense when things were not right.

Bradford motioned for him to come nearer. "Don't look so worried, Raphael. Everything's just fine. Your mother and I had a little difference of opinion but she's come around and it's all taken care of now."

Rose smiled at her son to reassure him but her glance at her husband said, we're not through with this one, Bradford. Nor will I encourage you to teach Rafe that a woman's opinions are unimportant and to be ignored.

The call came just as the family was finishing dinner. "What is it, Rose? What's the matter?"

"That was dad. Grandma Marsh died an hour ago."

It's about time! Bradford thought with satisfaction. *That old witch never did like me. Her beady eyes followed me around like a vulture every time we were around her. She sure didn't know how to treat a man!*

"I'm sorry mama," said Raphael. "Don't feel bad. She's up in heaven now, isn't she?"

"Yes, sweetheart." She hugged him as the tears rolled freely down her cheeks. "I'm sure of that. I'm not feeling bad for her. I'm feeling bad cause I'll miss her. She was always so good to me."

Rose glanced at Bradford, noting the flush on his face and the hateful expression in his eyes. With visible effort he tried to appear sympathetic.

"When's the funeral? I'll have to look at my schedule to see if we can make it."

Rose turned to Raphael, "Run upstairs and find a book for us to read, honey. I'll be up in a few minutes to give you your bath."

When she heard him reach the top of the stairs and go into his bedroom she turned with fury in her eyes and said between clenched teeth, "Bradford, I don't give a damn whether you can find time or not. Rafe and I are going to Creekston. And I'm not waiting until the day of the funeral, either."

He was astounded. He had never heard such steel in her voice. For the first time in his life he couldn't find words. He stood with his mouth open.

She looked at him sadly. "Don't worry about it. I've always known how you felt about my grandmother. And I saw how you looked just now. You don't have to worry about finding time to go with us. I'll make excuses for you." She turned wearily away.

He reached out to touch her, then pulled his hand back. He would not take orders from her! "You can go, Rose, but you're not taking Raphael with you."

She stopped and turned around slowly. "To use one of your favorite expressions, I don't want to discuss it." She turned her back on him and climbed the stairs.

* * *

Raphael loved kindergarten. He loved the stories and games and enjoyed playing with the other children. Every day he waited happily for the teacher to distribute the paper and crayons. Every afternoon he proudly took his work out to the car to show Rose. He didn't notice the growing coolness between his parents. He was happy so they must be happy, too.

* * *

Three weeks before school started the following year Rose said quietly to Bradford, "We need to talk."

He looked at her with exasperation. Why did this silly woman have to interrupt him every time he was in the middle of something important. "What is it?" he asked crossly.

"I'll be back as soon as I've finished putting Raphael to bed." She saw his frown but held her ground. "Don't worry, it won't take long."

Forty-five minutes later Rose shut the door carefully and sat on the sofa. Bradford put his papers down with an aggrieved sigh. "All right. I'm listening. Let's get this over with."

"Bradford, do you remember last year when I talked about going back to teaching?"

"Of course I remember. It was an idiotic idea."

"No, it was a good idea. But I didn't want the trouble between us to intensify so I didn't press." She hurried on, "My feelings haven't changed. Dean Walker called a few days ago and told me one of the teachers had to resign because of health problems and offered me his classes. I accepted."

"You what!?"

"You heard me. I'm going back to my teaching job at the U."

"Well just call him back and tell him you can't!"

"No. I won't do that because I am going to teach. Raphael will be in school all day this year. I'll not be neglecting him or you by teaching part time."

His face was suffused with anger now and he had to restrain himself from striking her. "You will do as I say! Do you understand? You will not work!"

She sat very still, knowing that if she gave in to him this time her remaining sense of self worth would be destroyed for good.

"I don't want to quarrel about this, Bradford. I am going to teach. Classes don't start for six weeks but I'm telling you now so you can get used to the idea."

"You've not heard the last of this," he said as he turned away.

The following week she received a call from Dean Walker saying how sorry he was she would be unable to teach after all.

"What? What are you talking about?"

He was mystified. "I've got your letter of refusal right here in front of me. I have to admit I'm surprised. I was looking forward to having you in the department again. But I do understand if you can't."

Very quietly she said, "Read the letter to me, please."

Thoroughly confused now, he read the brief paragraph over her signature stating that she wouldn't be able to teach after all because of previous commitments.

After a pause Rose said, "Dean, I didn't write that letter. Someone seems to be playing a practical joke on us." She didn't add that she knew who that someone was.

He laughed. "Well, I'm certainly relieved to hear that. And," he added wryly, "whoever played that joke has a strange sense of humor."

"Yes," she replied, "but let's not worry about it. Please remember, though, that if you receive any other resignations like that, they're not from me so just ignore them."

"I will. I will. See you at the meeting on the thirteenth." They hung up.

So you're going to play those games, Bradford, she thought. *Well, this time I won't talk to you about it. I'll just do what I have to do.*

It was the middle of the term before Bradford realized

Rose was teaching after all. He was furious but she remained adamant. She had proven, she told him, that her teaching did not interfere in any way with their family life. She hoped that would end the dispute.

Bradford didn't bring it up again and their lives continued as before, he uncommunicative and she pretending nothing was wrong so that Raphael would not be pulled into the middle of their differences.

The day before the term ended Rose picked up the mail and sorted through it. There were the usual invitations, business letters to Bradford and junk mail. And there was a manila envelope addressed to Mr. and Mrs. B. Stewart. Rose opened it wondering if it was more junk mail.

She couldn't believe her eyes. Raphael had been accepted to the Maple Valley Military Academy next fall and enclosed were the rules and regulations he would be following for the next eleven years.

It didn't make any sense at all. She read the cover letter again, and then a third time. Finally the message registered. Bradford had enrolled Raphael in the school in Massachusetts without saying a word to her.

That night after Raphael was asleep, Rose quietly laid the envelope on the desk where Bradford was working. He sputtered, "What are you doing opening my mail?"

Her voice was deadly calm. "If you'll look, you'll see it's addressed to Mr. AND Mrs. How could you do such a thing, Bradford?"

He turned away. "He's my son, Rose, and he's going to attend the same academy I did."

"You were twelve years old when your parents sent you there."

"It doesn't matter. Seven is a good age. Raphael will get a better start by going younger."

"A better start for what? Controlling people's lives? Learning to be dogmatic? Making decisions without consulting others?"

Her quiet calm unnerved Bradford. "What the hell are you talking about? Going to Maple Valley will be the best thing that'll ever happen to Raphael!"

"Even better than marrying and having his own children?"

"Yes," he caught himself, "No. You know what I mean."

"No, I don't know what you mean. All I know is that you made a decision about our son without including me."

"Well you took him to your grandmother's funeral when I specifically told you not to. And you went back to teaching when I specifically told you not to."

"And you think this is the same thing?"

Again he stumbled. "Yes. No. The reasoning is the same."

"Help me understand, Bradford. You're planning to send Raphael away to school to pay me back for decisions I made without your approval?"

He began to pace. "Approval has nothing to do with it. I know what's best for my son and I intend to do it."

Rose stepped in front of Bradford causing him to face her. "No, Bradford. Your decision not to have more children was made without my consideration. But you will not make a decision about sending Raphael away to school without including me." Her voice hardened, "If the time ever comes that we both think Raphael will benefit by going away to a military academy, we'll decide together. In the meantime, Raphael will not be going back east to school next year."

As she turned to leave the room his words came coldly to her. "You stand in my way Rose and I'll divorce you. I swear I will."

She turned around. "I don't think so, Bradford. That would ruin your hopes for the gubernatorial race next election."

Now his voice was murderous. "You'll pay for your insubordination, Rose. I'll make sure of that!"

Without responding she left the room and closed the door quietly behind her.

Military school was not discussed again but Rose remained wary knowing Bradford would not forget or forgive her interference in his plans for their son.

She thought long and hard about the superficiality of their marriage. She knew this was not the way marriage was meant to be. Nearly all marriages have ups and downs, good times and bad but theirs was nearly untenable. Yet the alternative was unthinkable. To leave Bradford would mean a vicious custody battle which she was afraid would do irreparable harm to Raphael. No, maybe when Rafe was older and could handle it, but not now. Now she would forge ahead working to keep her own self esteem intact while she continued to help Rafe strengthen his.

So Rose continued to selflessly support her husband in his determination to get the party's bid for the next Governor's race, attending numerous meetings and being a gracious hostess whenever Bradford invited party bigwigs to their home.

Bradford gave little thought to Rose's efforts to maintain an outwardly happy home life. He would give her another couple of years to get used to the idea of sending Raphael away to military school, then he would work fast to accomplish the deed before Rose realized what he was doing.

He was sure he could bring her around to his way of thinking eventually. She might think she was demonstrating her independence by teaching but that was trivial in comparison to his future plans. And Rose's place in those plans became dimmer each time she defied him. When the time was right, he would phase her out of the picture and find someone to be a real help meet.

But for now, Rose was still an asset. Her beauty and personality awed the party chairman and his co-workers, prompting Bradford to make full use of her talents. His manipulative skills were evident in every newspaper photograph and TV image where he was always pictured with his arm around Rose's waist or smiling devotedly at her. His charm and her beauty were irresistible.

However, once his political future was secure he would work out a way to replace her. He had studied national political figures until he was sure he could work the system as skillfully as they did. He might even be able to create a situation that would cause such an outpouring of sympathy and support for him he would be a natural for the next big step. Two years until the top state race, then one term in office and on to higher national aspirations.

* * *

"Hi, mom. It's great to hear from you. How are you and dad?"

"Just fine, Rose, just fine. In fact," Bess chuckled, "we're doing so well we're going on a medical mission."

"You are? Where?"

"Hold on to your hat. We're going to Romania."

"Romania! Why Romania?"

"Since the breakup of the regime there they're for all the help they can get. And since dad and I are both medically qualified, we figured this would be a good way to begin our retirement."

"Romania," Rose repeated. "That'll take some getting used to for me."

"For us, too. But once we made up our minds, everything seemed to fall into place."

"When do you leave?"

"September seventh."

Rose looked at the calendar. Two months from now. "How long will you be gone?"

"We had our choice between eighteen months and two years but we figured if we were going to go all that way, we just as well stay the full two years."

"I'll miss you. But as it's starting to sink in I have to say I think it'll be wonderful and a blessing for those poor people. Is your Farewell scheduled yet?"

"Yes. It's set for the last Sunday in August. You'll be here, won't you?"

"Wild horses couldn't keep me away."

"That's good sweetheart because we want you to give the opening prayer. And we'd like Rafe to sing 'I Am a Child of God.' Do you think he'll do that?"

"Why don't you ask him yourself. He's right here."

Rose watched with pride as Raphael talked to his grandmother. He was tall for his eight years and had a quiet, affable manner that made it easy for others to love and respect him. Rose wasn't surprised when he agreed to sing.

The summer passed quickly. Rose and Raphael tried to talk Bradford into joining them on their frequent excursions around the valley but he was always too busy.

He did agree to go with them to her parents' Farewell, though. Rose wasn't sure whether it was because he really wanted to go or because he figured it would help his public image to appear to be a doting family man. In either case he was courteous to her family and pleasant to be around.

I wish it could be like this all the time, she thought, as she watched him visit easily with her cousins Lucyann and Trish. They were obviously taken in by his charm and told Rose later how lucky she was to be married to such a good man. She didn't have the heart to tell them his political campaign was already underway for next year.

* * *

"So, how do you like Utah, Ben?"

"You've got some spectacular scenery here. I've been here before to ski so I already knew about your 'greatest snow on earth.' But last month I took a trip into your Canyonlands and redrock areas. I've never seen anything like it."

Rose smiled, "I'm pretty impressed with it, too, and I grew up with it. Our family took trips into central and southern Utah every summer."

"Lucky you. I certainly intend to go back as soon as possible."

"Have you gone into the High Uintas or Flaming Gorge areas?"

"Not yet. That's my goal for next summer."

They were sitting in the faculty lounge enjoying their break between classes. Ben Dumont had arrived at the University of Utah last fall. This was his first teaching post since receiving his doctorate.

"There is one thing I'm confused about," he broke the comfortable silence, "I was warned to steer clear of you Mormons."

"And?" Rose laughed.

"I haven't yet discovered what it is I'm supposed to steer clear of."

"You mean you don't find us strange?"

"Not only do I not find you strange, most of the Mormons I've met are downright friendly."

"Well," she responded, "You'll find as you meet more of us that we're just like people everywhere. Some of us are friendly, some of us are perverse and some of us range all the way between those two poles."

"I'm beginning to sense that. That's why I can't figure what the warnings were about."

"You're from the Bible Belt, aren't you?"

"Yes."

"Well, I've met a few people from there and for some reason they didn't seem to think we're Christians."

"Yes, I heard that. But I visited church with the department head and his family a couple of times and it seemed to me the prayers always ended 'in the name of Jesus Christ.' So why the discrepancy?"

"Good question," Rose answered, "I haven't a clue. Maybe someone else has figured that out but I've got other things to work on before I start delving into that." She stood up, "Including getting back to my next class."

Ben arose, too, and headed toward his classroom. He had noticed the strained look on Rose's face sometimes and concluded she had things on her mind that were troubling her. But it wasn't in his nature to pry. Just being on friendly terms with her was enough.

* * *

Letters from Rose's parents arrived regularly through the winter. Their major responsibilities were trying to improve the conditions and health of the orphans in Bucharest. Although their letters dwelled on the positive aspects of their work, Rose learned of the other side from the news media. Heartbreaking reports came of the inhumane conditions which had existed under the socialist dictatorship of Nicole Ceausescu and his cruel wife. Rose was saddened by the news and grateful her parents were able to help there. Their letters always included how glad they were to hear things were going well with her.

How I wish I could tell them the truth, Rose thought as she read. But it was out of the question. She didn't want to burden them with her situation.

She couldn't put her finger on what was occurring but a subtle change had come over Bradford. He was polite and even attentive when others were around but was inexorably and steadily shutting her out of his life. She tried to talk to him about it but he told her she was being neurotic. *Am I?* she wondered. *Am I imagining things?*

Bradford smiled grimly as he watched Rose grow more unsure of herself. His scheme was going according to schedule. He had known it would if he just played his cards right. The first step was to undermine her confidence in herself. He was already seeing results in this area.

The next step was to deliberately turn Raphael against her. It was time to begin this campaign. Once that was accomplished he could take the final step - removing her physically from his life once his political future was secure.

Although he had not been involved in Raphael's transportation in previous years, Bradford now offered to take turns picking him up from school. Rose was uncomfortable with this change but could see no justifiable reason why she should not be in agreement. As the weeks passed, whenever Bradford took his turn Raphael seemed restless and irritable in the evening.

"Is anything the matter, sweetheart?" Rose finally asked as she kissed Rafe good night.

Raphael looked at her strangely. "No." He paused. "Do you like me?"

She was astounded. "I love you, Rafe! How can you even ask such a question?"

"If you really love me, why do you work?"

She held him tenderly waiting for his tense body to relax. "Does it bother you that I work, Rafe?"

"It didn't used to. But sometimes I wonder if you love your job more than you love me and that's why you don't pick me up every day like you used to."

A terrible suspicion was growing in Rose's mind. "What makes you think that, sweetie?"

"Nothing," he muttered, turning away, "I don't want to talk about it anymore." She was dumbfounded. These were not the words of a child.

"All right. But before we stop just tell me when you started to wonder if I love you."

He blurted out, "Well, sometimes dad asks me if I think you love me as much as he does. And sometimes he buys me a treat on the way home. You never do that."

No, she thought as she walked quietly out of the room, *I don't teach my son to question his father's love. Nor do I stop on the way home for treats. Bradford has always insisted that sweets would spoil dinner for a growing boy. And, stupid me, I agreed.*

Rose watched Bradford's complacent smile as he worked through his papers the rest of the evening. She wasn't ready to confront him about Rafe yet. She had some hard thinking of her own to do first.

Rose made it a point to stop for Raphael after school every afternoon after that. When Bradford questioned her she said she had more time now that midterms were over. Gradually the apprehensive look Raphael had acquired faded from his eyes.

"Bradford, did anything come from mother and dad?"

"No."

That's unusual, Rose thought, *their letters were coming so regular and now I haven't received anything for over a month. I wonder if they're all right.*

She went into the bedroom and called Creekston. "Hi, Aunt Martha. Have you heard from mom and dad recently?"

"Yes. I got a letter about ten days ago and another one yesterday. Why?"

"I'm not sure. I haven't heard from them for awhile."

"Maybe the mail got mixed up."

"Yes," said Rose slowly, "maybe. Are they okay?"

"They're fine. Don't worry, Rosie dear, you'll probably get a handful of letters one of these days."

Maybe. But something is definitely wrong here. And I'm going to get to the bottom of it.

The following day Rose drove home at noon. She always ate lunch in her office so she wouldn't have to bring papers home to correct but today she wanted to be home when the mail arrived.

Bradford's car was in the driveway. Perplexed, she pulled her car in and parked beside his. Bradford had declared often that he was too busy to come home in the middle of the day. What was he doing here now?

The front door was unlocked and when she stepped inside, the house was quiet. Still bewildered, she looked in the downstairs rooms then climbed slowly up the stairs. Their bedroom door was ajar. She pushed it open and saw Bradford standing with his back to her, placing letters in a shirt box.

"Bradford? What are you doing home?"

He whirled around. "Where did you come from? I didn't hear you come in."

He tried to push the box back into the drawer but it caught on the edge and spilled it's contents onto the floor.

Rose saw letters with her mother's handwriting on them and a large envelope with the crest of Maple Valley Military Academy on the front.

"What are you doing, Bradford? Where did these letters come from?"

She reached down and picked up a letter from the floor. The postmark said Rumania. She picked up four more just like it and holding them tightly in shaking hands walked slowly out the door.

Bradford was at her side instantly, his face glowering down at her. "What the hell are you doing here, Rose?" he asked coldly.

"I might ask you the same thing," she held up the letters, "and what are you doing with my letters? Don't bother to answer. Nothing you could say would excuse what you've done."

"I've done exactly what I promised you I'd do! I've made you pay for defying me!"

"Defying?" she asked in confusion.

"Oh yes, my dear wife," his voice was like ice. "I told you you'd pay for interfering with my plans for Raphael." He watched her eyes widen as the memory flooded back. "This time you're too late to stop me."

The military school . . . the large envelope . . . She looked at him in horror. "What have you done?"

"Exactly what I told you I'd do. I've completed the arrangements for my son's future. He leaves for Massachusetts in the morning." His eyes were filled with venom.

"No!" she cried, grabbing his arm, "I'll stop you!"

"Try," he laughed triumphantly, "it won't do you any

good. He wants to go!" He shoved her away from him.

She flew at him fiercely, all the anger and frustration she had felt for so long finally surfacing. Her strength was no match for his. He forced her slowly to the top of the stairs.

Realizing what his intention was, Rose grabbed the banister and cried, trying to reason with him, "Don't Bradford! Think about your good name!"

Prying her fingers loose he laughed maliciously, "My good name will remain intact. The public will be filled with sorrow as I grieve over my personal tragedy. I'll garner even more votes."

With that he gave Rose a vicious shove. Her hands flailed the air trying to find something to hold onto. Her fingers closed desperately around one of the staircase balusters, stopping the momentum of her fall. At the same time her feet flew into the air, becoming entangled with Bradford's legs. With a cry of enraged surprise, he rolled head over heels down the stairs, coming to rest at the bottom.

Rose clung to the baluster, her eyes tightly closed. Through the roaring in her head she heard him crawl back up, one step at a time, his breathing engulfed in rasping gasps. She knew she had to open her eyes and run but didn't have the strength to do so.

After what seemed to be an eternity, Rose realized the terrible rasping sound was her own breathing. Slowly she opened her eyes. Bradford lay at the bottom of the staircase, his head at an awkward angle. Cautiously she started down the stairs toward him.

* * *

Reporters jostled each other as they waited in front of the Stewart home. Rose and Raphael couldn't leave the house without running a gauntlet of questions.

"Was your husband's fall an accident, Mrs. Stewart?"

"Raphael, is it true your father was leaving your mother?'

"Are the accusations by your in-laws true, Mrs. Stewart? Did you push your husband to his death?"

"Rose? This is Ben Dumont. What can I do to help?"

"Oh Ben, there's nothing anyone can do. We've just got to ride this out." She added, "Thanks for calling. And please tell the others how much I appreciate their support."

"We're all behind you, Rose. We're appalled at what's happening to you and want you to know we're here if you need us."

"Thanks again, Ben. Rafe and I will be fine. I've been told to expect an announcement soon."

"This is Channel Six News. The autopsy shows that State Legislator Bradford J. Stewart, the man most mentioned for the governor's seat in the fall, died of a broken neck in an accident at his home. The Attorney General has cleared Rose Stewart of complicity in his death stating that there was no evidence to support the accusations of criminal homicide brought by Mr. Stewart's parents. They say they will take their case to the Supreme Court."

* * *

"I love you, mama. Please don't be sad any more."

Rose wiped her eyes. "My sweet Rafe, I don't know what I'd do without you. You've been such a..." Her comment was interrupted by the doorbell.

"I'll go," Raphael said quickly, "You stay here. I can take care of it."

"Thanks, Rafe." She took his hand and forced herself to smile, "Let's take care of it together."

Rose looked through the security hole then quickly opened the door wide enough for Jay to slip through.

"We've been watching the news, Rose. Dad sent me to come and bring you and Rafe to Flagstaff until this blows over."

"Bless your hearts. We were starting to get cabin fever. Come on, Rafe, let's pack and get out of here." She turned back to Jay, "Where are you parked?"

"Down on the corner."

"Good. We can slip out the back door and down the alley and be on our way before those reporters out in front realize we're gone."

She threw her arms around him then looked down at Raphael who was grinning from ear to ear. "Thanks, Jay. I can't tell you how much we appreciate this."

He smiled warmly, "There's nothing to thank me for. I would have come sooner but we knew you couldn't leave until things were cleared up. Now, get your things together and let's get this show on the road and not keep dad waiting any longer."

Chapter Eleven

Letting Go

Saturday, August 10th, 12:10 p.m.

Duane studied Rose thoughtfully. "Are you and Rafe okay now?"

"Yes," she answered quietly. "The first few weeks back were hard but things have pretty well settled down now." She laughed, "Thank heavens the media people have found new interests."

"What happened about Bradford's parents and their threat to go to the Supreme Court?"

"They dropped it after a couple of news articles appeared questioning their motives and their son's good name. I think they realized, too, that they might lose contact with Rafe if they continued to attack me. They're still stand-offish to me but they do love Rafe and know that the only way they can see him is to include me, too."

"How do you feel about them?"

Rose took Duane's hand. "The time I spent with you in Flagstaff helped me let go of all the anger and frustration. You helped me see that carrying that baggage around would only pull me down with it." She smiled, "And Rafe thinks the sun rises and sets in you. You were exactly what he need-ed at that point in his life."

Duane patted her hand. "I'm glad. And I'm glad that you're learning to put it behind you." He added, "Your stay was good for me, too. Just remember you two are welcome any time you want to come."

They sat in comfortable silence, enjoying each other's company. Then Melissa asked, "What about that Professor Dumont you said was so helpful? Is he still in Salt Lake?"

Rose's face glowed with pleasure. "Yes. He's on a camping trip in the High Uintas this month but will be back in a couple of weeks."

Duane smiled inwardly, glad to see Rose's expression. *She is really letting go of the heartache and getting on with her life,* he thought. *That's good. That's what this life is all about—getting past the sorrows and going toward the joy.* He was glad to have lived long enough to learn that.

Chapter Twelve

Duane

He turned slowly from side to side trying to capture all the incredible colors within his view. The sky was a clear, gentle blue and the green on which he stood glimmered with emerald lights as far as he could see. Flowers were profuse, more beautiful than he had ever seen and trees stood in stately splendor, dappling the ground with dancing hues.

In the distance he watched as a man encircled in brilliant light moved toward him, arms extended in welcome. He waited calmly for their encounter.

"Welcome. It's good to have you home again, Duane."

"Thank you. I'm delighted to finally get here."

"How was your journey?"

Duane smiled. "Most interesting. My experiences varied from the greatests heights to the deepest depths. But," he added, "I wouldn't have missed any of them."

"ANY of them?"

Duane paused. "Well, at the time they were happening I didn't always appreciate them. Once or twice I even wondered where I could hand in my resignation. Yet even during the worst times, I did learn something." He continued wryly, "Although sometimes the wisdom didn't come until long after the experience had ended."

He smiled, "That's the way with wisdom. It needs thought and time and deliberation. Wisdom comes in many shapes and forms but is there to be found for those who seek it."

"Yes," Duane said, "I was beginning to comprehend that before I left." He looked around thoughtfully, "It's interesting how very peaceful it is here. There are no feelings of sorrow. Or of stress," he added.

"You are aware that many times stress is self inflicted, aren't you?"

"I am now. But I didn't know it during the first part of my journey." Duane sighed, "It took a lot of hard knocks and some terrible times for me to learn to separate what really matters from trivial concerns."

"For example?"

"Well," Duane said slowly, "Learning to understand the true meaning of agency was a life-long process. I finally did come to realize that each of us is answerable for our own actions and we have to live with the consequences of those actions. And, too, I learned that there aren't always simple solutions for complex problems."

Duane paused, deep in thought as the memories flooded back. Quietly he continued, "After many years I came to understand that people aren't always asking for easy solutions. Sometimes all they want is someone to understand how they're feeling. It's too bad it takes so long to learn how to listen with the heart."

"Yes. 'They have ears but hear not.' When did you come to this realization?"

"I'm not sure exactly. It was a gradual process of realizing that it wasn't necessary to have all the answers, only necessary to care. I finally came to know that, though I couldn't cure the world of turmoil, I could rid myself of my own personal demons of intolerance and censure."

"I'm glad you came to that understanding. Some never do."

"I learned also," Duane said slowly, "that pure joy

doesn't come from material things. It comes when we realize our relationships with one another are too vital to be taken lightly. Being truly concerned for the happiness and well-being of another is so much more important than power or treasures. When we all become partners, true children of God, nothing else counts for much.

"Loving our neighbor as ourself isn't an empty phrase. It means exactly what it says. This, I now know, is the overriding lesson of life. This is what really matters."

"Yes," he smiled warmly, "you've learned well in your sojourn on earth, Duane. Come with me now. They're all waiting for you."

They walked up the gentle incline until they were at the top of a small rise. There before them were crowds of people, smiling expectantly.

Peering closer into their faces, Duane recognized his beloved mother and father, and Jess, Ralph, Everett, Rafe, Rudy, Lulabelle and all the others who had meant so much to him.

A single figure separated from the group and walked joyfully toward him, her arms outstretched in love.

"Lucinda! My darling Lucinda! I've missed you so," Duane exclaimed as he hurried into her waiting arms.